THE TIME-TRAVELLING CAT
and the
AZTE

Other Titles by Julia Jarman

THE TIME-
TRAVELLING CAT
and the
AZTEC SACRIFICE

JULIA JARMAN

Andersen Press • London

To the wonderful librarians at Stockport SLS.
'One for the Aztec box!'

First published in 2006 by
Andersen Press Limited,
20 Vauxhall Bridge Road, London SW1V 2SA

www.andersenpress.co.uk

© 2006 Julia Jarman

British Library Cataloguing in Publication Data available

ISBN 10: 1 84270 516 4
ISBN 13: 978 1 84270 516 2

Typeset by FiSH Books, Enfield, Middx.
Printed and bound in Great Britain by Bookmarque Ltd., Croydon, Surrey

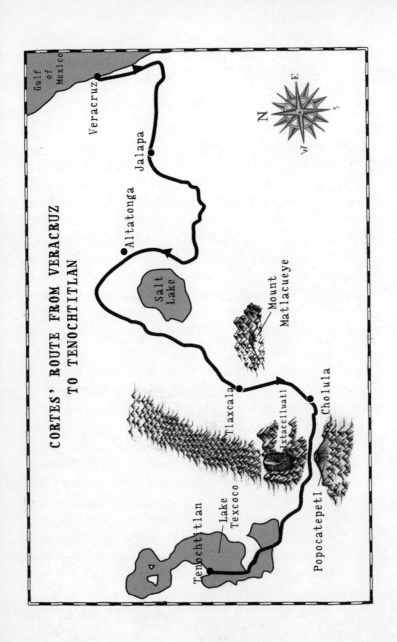

CORTES' ROUTE FROM VERACRUZ
TO TENOCHTITLAN

Gulf
of
Mexico

Veracruz

Jalapa

Altatonga

Salt
Lake

Mount
Matlacueye

Tlaxcala

Ixtacciluatl

Cholula

Lake
Texcoco

Tenochtitlan

Popocatepetl

N
E
W
S

Chapter 1

'Don't ever travel to the time of the Aztecs, Ka.'

Topher Hope ran his fingers through his cat's silky fur.

'I'd hate to have to go there.' He was watching, well half-watching, a programme about the Aztecs, and they were making a blood sacrifice. It wasn't real blood, he told himself, as he studied Ka's golden fur flecked with black and white. That was paint pouring down the pyramid steps. But the Aztecs did sacrifice people. Everyone knew that. They thought the sun wouldn't rise if they didn't kill someone every day in exactly the same way. They didn't dare make the slightest change. They were dead against change. Dead was the word.

Ka's fur crackled and clung to his fingers as he stroked her – static electricity. Outside a crust of snow covered the grass. As he glanced out of the window – it was dark but no one had closed the curtains – Topher thought about all the changes in his life, some good some bad. His mum dying had been very bad. His dad meeting then marrying Molly had seemed bad, but turned out good. Moving house and leaving his best friend, Ellie, in London had been bad. He'd moved house twice now. But keeping in touch with Ellie was good and finding Ka – or had she found him? – was very, very good. He stroked her throat and felt her purring beneath his fingers.

1

'Did you hear me, Ka? Don't travel to the time of the Aztecs.'

Ka was a time-travelling cat, though only Topher knew that, because he travelled with her sometimes. She turned to face him so he could see her amber eyes, and the ankh on her forehead. The glossy black key-like mark was the Egyptian sign of life. She'd been to Ancient Egypt several times.

Don't wo-rrr-y. Don't wo-rrr-y. She seemed to speak, sometimes did speak. The commentator had started talking about sacrifices and he turned down the sound. When they'd done the Aztecs at school, he'd laughed at stuff like that, but now it didn't seem so funny – especially with Tallulah crying. Tally, as they mostly called her, was his new baby sister, nearly a year old now, and she was upstairs in her cot. She'd been bawling when he switched on the TV a quarter of an hour ago. That was why he'd put it on. He couldn't bear to hear her cry, and luckily she didn't much. She was usually so happy. She made him laugh, and he made her laugh. He'd been surprised to discover how entertaining a baby could be. If she did cry she nearly always stopped when someone gave her a cuddle or a feed. But not tonight. She was still crying, though Molly and his dad were with her. He turned the sound up again.

At least the gruesome bits seemed to be over. The voice-over was saying that the Aztecs didn't have cows, sheep or goats, and therefore no cheese, butter or milk.

'You wouldn't like that, Ka.' She loved creamy milk and her favourite treat was a cube of cheese. 'But I suppose you could eat rabbit or turkey meat – or dog.'

They had strange wrinkled hairless dogs and tiny hairy ones called Chihuahuas, but they didn't have horses or cats, well not domestic cats. That was a relief. Ka probably wouldn't go there.

'But if you do you must tell me.'

Of cou ... rrrse. Of cou ... rrrse.

She sometimes told him where she'd been by pressing the keyboard of his computer and writing a word. She was extraordinarily clever. 'But I'm not sure if you could spell the names of Aztec places. They're weird.'

She frowned as if to say, *I'm not stupid.*

'Okay, but if you're thinking of going tell me, right, before you go?'

He didn't say – so I can persuade you not to. Try, anyway. Ka had a mind of her own, like all cats. She didn't obey or do tricks like a dog.

'Did you hear me?'

She didn't reply. In fact she turned to face the TV as the voice-over described what Aztecs ate. They had sweet corn, peppers, tomatoes and beans, including cocoa beans.

'Not much there for you, Ka, except chocolate.'

Chocolate was her second favourite treat.

'Chocolate? Did someone say chocolate?' said Molly from the doorway. She must have crept downstairs. 'Shall I make some?'

'No, you sit down.' His dad stood behind her now, glasses on top of his bald head.

'I'll get it.'

Topher and his dad had the same name – Christopher Hope – so to avoid confusion, his dad was called Chris for short, and Topher was called Topher. That had been his mum's idea. As Chris Hope went off to the kitchen Molly flumped down beside Topher, and pushed back her black hair.

'What was the matter with Tally?'

'Not sure. Probably a cold.'

'As long as she's not ill?'

'Don't think so.' Molly gave him a hug. 'You love her, don't you? Everyone told me you'd be jealous.'

'Everyone told *me* I'd be jealous.' He laughed. 'Perhaps that's why I'm not.'

Next day, a Saturday, he made a snowman for Tally. The good thing about the house in Chichester was the huge garden. It had a pond with willow trees dangling in it, and ducks and moorhens and lots of other birds. Tally laughed and pulled the carrot nose off the snowman's face, struggling to get free from Molly, though she couldn't walk yet.

Topher said, 'She seems happiest outside.'

'Yes. I think she finds it easier to breathe. I'm beginning to wonder if she's allergic to something in the house.'

'Like what?'

'House dust's the commonest cause.'

Or cat hair. The words came into Topher's head.

'If it is,' Molly went on, 'we'll have to become super-clean. I've asked Georgio to give her room a thorough going over.'

4

'I wondered why he was here today.'

Georgio was their cleaning-man, an actor at the local theatre, who also worked for Merry Maids, the cleaners. He usually came on a weekday when everyone was out.

'Look there he is.' Molly pointed to an upstairs window. 'Look, Tally, there's Georgio. Wave.'

She waved and a dark-haired young man waved back, and Topher saw Ka sitting in the conservatory, bird-watching. Zingi, her son, a fluffy ginger kitten, sat beside her. Both cats had started to come outside with him, but changed their minds when they felt the snow under their paws. Topher felt uneasy. He couldn't help thinking about a boy at school who'd been allergic to cats. They gave him asthma and he'd had to find his cat a new home. Finding a new home for Ka was too awful to think about. So why was he thinking about it? Nobody had said anything about asthma, or cat hair, or getting rid and Tally seemed fine now. She was clapping her hands and shrieking, making birds fly into the air.

What had Ellie said once – 'For someone called Hope you haven't got much, have you?' It was when Ka had first gone missing – before he knew she was a time-travelling cat. He'd been pessimistic again when Ellie went into hospital for an operation. Ellie had yelled at him, 'Topher, HOPE!' He had, and her operation had been successful. So he decided to be hopeful now. Tally would be fine.

But soon after they went back inside, when they were sitting in the conservatory having a snack, she started coughing and sneezing. She went red in the face and when a drink didn't calm her down Molly looked round and caught sight of Ka and Zingi on the windowsill – and her expression changed.

Topher went rigid. He knew what she was thinking. He'd been watching the cats, still now, with their paws tucked beneath them. But only a few moments before Zingi had been scratching behind his ear, and hairs flew off him. Now they were floating upwards in a little cloud. That's what Molly was watching.

She said, 'I wonder...' and walked out of the conservatory holding Tallulah close.

Topher thought, Hope, *hope*, but felt his heart sinking.

Chapter 2

At lunch his dad said that the cats must live outside. All of them – Ka and Zingi and Buggins the old fat tabby who had been Molly's before she married his dad. Nowadays Buggins spent most of his time sleeping in a box next to the boiler in the laundry room.

'But it's January!' Topher protested as they carried box and bedding to the back of the garage. 'There's snow on the ground!'

'We'll buy them a shelter.' His dad didn't even allow a discussion. 'Today.'

'We aren't even sure if cat hair is upsetting Tally. She's probably got a cold.'

'This way we'll find out, see if she's better when the cats live outside.'

'You're supposed to do allergy tests.'

'This is a test, Topher. We don't want doctors sticking needles in her unless we have to.'

He couldn't argue with that.

They went to a garden centre and bought a shed, a *shed*, for Ka who loved warmth and comfort. She had just started sleeping on Topher's bed again. When she'd had kittens to feed she'd slept with them downstairs in a basket. Now the basket was Zingi's. Chris Hope was optimistic that making the cats live outside would solve Tallulah's problem. 'They *are* cats,' he said as if Topher didn't know.

That night Topher couldn't get to sleep for worrying. The cats were in the garage because the shed hadn't been delivered yet. As he lay awake, watching the luminous hands of his bedside clock, he kept checking that the statue of Ka wasn't there, hoping it wasn't there – because if it was it meant Ka was time-travelling. The statue was exactly like Ka, carved from sardonyx, a honey-coloured stone with black and white flecks. His mum had brought it back from Egypt, and given it to him before she died. When Ka went time-travelling the statue stayed behind. It was as if she left behind a replica of herself to remind him what she looked like. As if he could forget! And when she was coming back from her travels the statue seemed to smoulder and burst into life. Seemed? No it *did* burst into life in the most amazing way. It *became* Ka. You had to see it to believe it. There was no point in trying to describe it to anyone.

He put on the light and looked under the bed, because sometimes he'd found it at different places in his room – in the place where she'd vanished from, he supposed. He didn't know because he'd never seen her go. But he didn't search for long, because he didn't really want to find it. So he put out the light and told himself she was okay, safe in the garage. But she must hate being locked up. She hated being confined. She hated litter trays and cold. Surely she wouldn't stand it for long? Why would she stay outside in a cold country when she could travel to Ancient Egypt and live in luxury? Or to Roman times, where she could live in a comfortable Roman villa? He remembered her, stretched out on a warm mosaic floor, where central heating pipes passed beneath.

He did eventually get to sleep but woke early. No statue. Ace. He got dressed and rushed out to the garage. Ka and Zingi were curled up together in their new basket, on a shelf at the back of the garage. They looked happy enough. He filled their dishes and they seemed even happier. Maybe things would turn out all right. Hope, Topher, *hope*.

The man from the garden centre spent most of Sunday putting up the shed, halfway down the garden, on a base of concrete slabs.

'Why can't they stay in the garage?' Topher asked his dad as they watched the man for a bit. 'At least that's warmer.' It was made of bricks.

'There's not room for the cats and two cars and all the stuff we keep there.'

'Couldn't the stuff go in the shed?'

'Topher, the cats will like the shed and they'll be able to get in and out by their cat flap.'

'They could have a cat flap in the garage.'

Chris Hope sighed. 'Topher, I don't want the cats climbing all over the cars. Didn't you see the scratches they've made already?'

'But...'

'Topher, enough!'

At lunch when he asked again, Molly said, 'I'm sorry, Topher, but Tally travels to nursery in my car every day. Let's keep her environment as cat free as we can and see what difference it makes.'

It was late afternoon and beginning to get dark before

the shed was ready. The man put up shelves so the cats could sleep above the ground. Topher made it as comfortable as he could – for the cats and himself. He hauled an old armchair down the garden and nailed an old velvet curtain over the door, but it still felt cold. There was no heating, no electricity supply even, and it was draughty.

'I'm sorry, Ka.' He was in the armchair and she was on his knee, purring.

It's all rrr-ight. It's all rrr-ight.

'You wouldn't like it in the house at the moment.'

Merry Maids were there in force. A whole team of cleaners, not just Georgio, were trying to get rid of any lingering cat hairs.

I underrr...stand. I underrr...stand.

'I think you do. You'd do anything to help Tally.' She was such a lovely cat. 'I still hope it's something else the matter with her, not you.'

Topher shone a torch on Buggins who was asleep in his box. His box and Zingi's basket were on the widest shelf. Topher had made a ramp so Buggins could get up and down. Ka and Zingi could both jump. Zingi had just gone outside, despite the snow on the ground. He liked to go hunting at night.

'I've got to go to school tomorrow, Ka. Will you be all right?'

Of courrr...se.

Of courrr...se.

Outside the wind whistled through the treetops. A screech owl called.

'The owl and Zingi are probably competing for mice. Don't you want to go hunting?'

Ka didn't. When Topher stood up she moved to the warm spot on the chair.

Later that night he lay listening to the wind. He glanced at his bedside table from time to time, but there was no sign of the statue. Ka probably was safe in her new bed. He got to sleep eventually but woke at first light worrying. *If Ka went time-travelling while she was in the shed, then wouldn't her statue be in the shed?* Full of foreboding he pulled on his school clothes. Then he raced downstairs and out to the shed.

Ka wasn't there, but the statue was – on the floor, on its side, near the dish.

She'd gone. Where had she gone? *When* had she gone *to*?

'What happened, Zingi?' The ginger cat was looking over the edge of the basket.

Buggins, still asleep, made no response.

'What happened, Zingi? Were you here? Did you see it? Did she tell you where she'd gone?'

He jumped down and rubbed round Topher's legs.

'Miaow!' Now he was looking at the packet of cat biscuits on the shelf, just like an ordinary cat. He showed no sign of having Ka's special powers.

Topher filled his dish and picked up the statue, the cold stone statue. He looked into its cold stone eyes. Stone eyes, not lustrous amber *alive* eyes whose pupils changed with the light.

11

'Come back, Ka.'

Should he leave it, *her*, where he'd found her, here in the shed? Or should he take her back to his bedroom? She had probably gone because she'd felt cold in the night. She had most likely gone *to* somewhere warm and comfortable. Wasn't she more likely to come back to somewhere warm and comfortable, where someone would take proper care of her?

He took the statue back to the house.

Molly was in the kitchen giving Tally her breakfast. Tally, her face covered with cereal, seemed perfectly well.

'Hi, Topher.' Molly laughed at Tally who was offering her a sticky spoon. 'Cats all right?'

'No. Ka isn't there.'

She didn't seem to hear.

He passed his father on the stairs.

'Morning, Topher.'

'Morning, Dad.'

'Where've you been?'

'To feed the cats, but Ka's gone.'

'Not to worry. She usually goes for a walk first thing. I hope you're not bringing any cat hair into the house.'

Neither of them commented on the statue in his hands.

Safe in his bedroom, Topher closed and locked the door. Luckily there was a lock. Tally couldn't be allergic to a statue surely? And if, *when*, Ka came back to life, well, he'd just have to keep Tally out of his room. He'd have to keep everyone out of his room. Did anyone else have a key? It might be best to hide the statue. Where? He opened the door of his bedside cupboard, and his nose filled with his mum's musky scent, from a scarf she used to wind round her long fair hair. His hair was the same colour. The scarf was flame coloured, red and orange and pink. For a long moment he held the scarf against his face and pictured his mum wearing it. Then he wrapped it round the statue, so only the face was peeping out, and changed his mind about putting it in the cupboard. Instead, he placed it carefully on top of the cupboard, between the lamp and the clock and whispered, 'Come back, Ka. Come back to me.'

But when he got home from school and raced upstairs to look, the house had an empty feeling – and the statue was still there. His dad and Molly were at work. Tally was in the nursery. *Good. This was all her fault.* No! He was surprised at the thought in his head. It wasn't Tally's fault. No point in blaming her. She hadn't decided that Ka and the other cats must live outside. She hadn't decided to be allergic to cats, if she was.

But he felt another twinge of resentment later in the evening. He needed help with his maths homework and Molly was upstairs fussing over Tally. Molly was ace at helping with homework. His dad was useless.

'You do know this, Topher.' He tapped the kitchen table impatiently.

'If I knew I wouldn't ask. What's the matter with Tally, anyway?'

Her crying wasn't helping.

'Not sure, but she's certainly not herself.'

'Despite banishing the cats.'

'I've been thinking about that. Wonder if you're still

13

bringing cat hair into the house. When you went to feed them this morning, did they rub round your legs like they usually do?'

'Ka didn't. She wasn't there. Still isn't.'

'But Zingi did? And then you walked into the house covered with his hairs?' He got up. 'I think I'll go and do a bit of cleaning.'

He wasn't worried about Ka obviously, or even the unfinished homework. Next thing he was mopping the kitchen floor. Then he got the hoover and headed for the stairs. But he was back moments later.

'Why's your bedroom door locked?'

In case Ka returns and wanders out of my room into the rest of the house. Of course he couldn't say that. *In case Ka returns and stays in my room but someone goes in and finds her.* He couldn't say that either.

'In case there are still a few hairs on my school trousers and Tally goes in.'

His dad nodded. 'Best go get them and put them in the washing machine. Here.' He gave Topher a plastic bag. 'Put them in this and bring them down. But hoover your bedroom first. I've left the cleaner upstairs. When you come down we'll have a think about how you're going to minimise contact with the cats.'

Minimise contact! Wasn't it minimal enough?

When Topher got back to the kitchen his dad said, 'That chair you took down to the shed, what's that for?'

'To sit on?' He couldn't help the sarcasm.

'With Ka on your knee? I thought so. And I bet she sleeps on the chair when you're not there. Better get the trousers you were wearing yesterday as well.'

'Would you like me to wear a bin bag?' More sarcasm, but his dad took him seriously!

'Something like that, over something you can keep in the shed. It's that, or find a new home for the cats.'

'Ka's probably found a new home for herself.'

And why would she want to come back? What sort of life would she have here?

As he switched out the light that night, Topher wasn't hopeful. He noticed that the scarf had slipped off. It lay like a pool of silk round the base of the statue, but he didn't notice the stone glowing.

Chapter 3

'Mwa.'

A tiny cry woke him, and he was sitting up in an instant. It was happening again. Ka was coming back! He saw her eyes gleaming. He saw circles of light on the wall opposite moving from left to right, right to left, and quickly turned back to face the statue. Face Ka – except that it wasn't her – not yet. But the stone was glowing, gleaming, shimmering like burning coal. It was happening. It was coming alive. But slowly, too slowly. He held his breath as hair by hair, tuft by tuft, stone became fur. Ears first, left then right, then forehead with the glossy ankh. Cheeks next and chin and – ah! – her mouth opened and closed.

'Mwa-a!' That was real enough. He saw her pink tongue and tiny white teeth.

'Mwa-aa!' The cry sounded painful, as if she were struggling to be born.

'Come on! Come on, Ka!'

He put out his hand and she turned her head towards it, so now he could see her amber eyes, wondrous amber rings of light round shiny black pupils. He saw her pink nose. Saw whiskers springing from her face. Now it really was Ka's face, furry and alive, but the rest of her was still like molten rock.

'Come on, Ka.'

Ripples ran through her, like a convulsion, but then her tail fluffed out in a rush, her back grew furry and so did her legs!

'Mwa!' *Touch me, Topher.*

He put out his hand, felt the hollow between her shoulder blades, felt bone beneath and warm, warm fur! She was furry all over now.

Downstairs the hall clock struck three.

He lifted the duvet and she leaped from the cupboard onto his bed. He felt her fur brush his stomach as she pull-pricked the bottom sheet with her claws, circling as she always did.

'Settle down, Ka.' He stroked her head as she snuggled down, tucking her paws beneath her and her eyes shone out of the dark cave. Then her eyes closed and he remembered to say, 'Welcome home' before they both fell into a contented sleep.

Chapter 4

'Topher! Topher!'

Someone was knocking on his bedroom door.

'TOPHER!'

His dad! Rattling the door handle now! Where was Ka? Ah – he lifted the duvet – there she was fast asleep.

His dad yelled again. 'It's seven o'clock! Why is this door locked? Get up or you'll be late for school!'

'I'm getting up.' Thank goodness he'd locked the door.

As he got out of bed Ka woke up. He stroked her head. 'Sorry, but you'd better get out of here.'

She understood and was on the windowsill before he had worked out the best exit.

'Of course. You're such a clever cat.' He opened the window and she leaped onto the conservatory roof below.

'At least the snow has melted.'

'Mwaw!' She looked back at him. *But I hate wet grass.*

Nevertheless she padded carefully to the edge of the roof and jumped off. Seconds later he saw her walking down the garden to the shed, picking up her paws and shaking them after each step.

'Ka's around. I've just seen her,' said Molly when he went down for breakfast.

'So have I – from my bedroom window,' he added,

when he saw his dad glaring at him.

Chris Hope looked at him over the top of his glasses. 'Locking your bedroom door isn't a good idea. What if there were a fire?'

'I'd open it.'

'There might not be time.'

'I'd climb out of my bedroom window then.'

'Onto the conservatory roof? I'm not sure it would take your weight – a cat's maybe but not yours.'

Was he suspicious? Luckily Tally distracted him with her favourite game.

'Boo!' said his dad as she covered her face with her bib and she shrieked with laughter.

'She's her normal cheerful self,' said Molly. 'It's good to see.'

When Topher got home from school he went straight to the shed. Ka was there, in the armchair, sleeping. She usually slept a lot after she'd been time-travelling.

'Where did you go, Ka?' He knelt down to speak to her face to face.

She woke and rubbed her cheek against his hand.

'Are you okay?'

He'd worried about her all day, felt bad because he hadn't examined her as soon as she got back. Once, when she'd been to Tudor times, she'd come back injured. Someone had tried to strangle her. She let him run his fingers through her fur, all over, feeling and looking for scratches or cuts.

I'm all rrr...ight. I'm all rrr...ight.

She was all right, but thirsty. Her milk and water dishes were empty.

'I'll fetch you some creamy milk.'

In the kitchen there was a note from his dad on the notice board.

TOPHER!
WEAR THIS COAT WHEN YOU'RE WITH THE CATS AND KEEP IT IN THE SHED.
DAD –>

He didn't even say please. The arrow pointed to a white coat hanging on the wall. It was an old lab coat of Molly's and reached his ankles. When he took the milk down to Ka, he had a moan about it, but she didn't seem bothered. *Be rrr...easonable. Be rrr...easonable.* Well, that's what her purring sounded like.

'So where did you go?' he asked again.

But all he could hear for the next few minutes was her lapping tongue.

He wanted to be reasonable. He wanted Tally to be well. Of course he did, so it might be a good idea to keep the house hair-free and see if that stopped her coughing and wheezing. If it didn't, well, something else must be the cause, and the cats could come back inside. If it did, well the price might be worth paying. Ka seemed to think so. She was purring now.

Co-operrr...ate. Co-operrr...ate. As she looked up at him, milk dropped from a little milk beard on her chin.

'Messy cat! But you're right.' He took off the lab coat and hung it on a nail. 'I'll double check I haven't brought any hairs into the house. You have a wash too. I'll be back as soon as I can.'

Molly had one of those sticky roller things for getting fluff and hairs off her clothes. He found it near the front door and gave himself a good going over. A few hairs came off. He rinsed the roller under the tap in the kitchen. Then he took it upstairs to his bedroom and rolled it over the sheet and duvet. It picked up a few hairs and a crumb or two – and a feather, a small bright red feather. He pulled it off the roller. Where did that come from? It was a shiny metallic red. What sort of bird had feathers like that? He put it in the top drawer of his desk, just below his computer.

Where had Ka been? Should he get her, put her in front of the computer and ask as he usually did? No. There would be more hairs to clean up. He had a better idea – if Molly hadn't taken her laptop to work.

She hadn't; it was in her study. He carried it down the garden, set it up on the shelf beside Ka's basket. And he put on the lab coat. He really was being co-operative.

'Just hope the batteries are charged up.'

Ka was outside the shed with Zingi, catching the last rays of the evening sun, but came in when he called.

'I hope you're as co-operative as me, Ka.'

Soon it would be dark. He must hurry. Buggins stirred and looked at them over the top of his box. Would Ka perform with an audience? Luckily Zingi was more interested in food, and as Topher lifted Ka onto the shelf, Buggins started to climb out of his box.

21

Ka studied the keyboard as Topher typed WHERE DID YOU GO?

'Where did you go? Understand?'

She looked disdainful.

'Answer me then – please,' he added.

She began to lick her paw.

Sometimes he thought she teased him.

'Please.'

She dangled one paw over the keyboard.

Then Buggins and Zingi had a spat, because Zingi was trying to steal from Buggins's dish. Buggins growled, but Zingi didn't take the hint. He pinched a piece of meat, so Buggins batted him, and Zingi fought back. Fur flew!

'Shoo! Out!' Topher chased Zingi into the garden.

When he came back Ka's right paw was still hovering over the keyboard and she had typed one letter.

Chapter 5

It was T. Or T ^^^ to be precise. Her paw must have hit the key above as well. The keyboard of the laptop was smaller than she was used to, but she did manage an E next.

Then she moved her paw to the bottom row of keys. T^^^ENB

'Tenby?' He'd been there once, to the seaside. But no, she pressed DELETE and typed O – and several bracket signs just above the O on the keyboard. But gradually a word, a strange word, took place.

TENO)) C . . . TENOC TENOCHT^ TENOCHTIT-LAN Not so strange. He'd seen it before. TENOCH-TITLAN. Wasn't that the name of an Aztec city? Worrying.

'Ka, the Aztecs didn't have cats.'

She looked at him scornfully.

He got onto the net and did a Google search for TENOCHTITLAN. It came up with a hundred and fifteen thousand references, but the first one told him he was right. It was the most famous Aztec city, built where Mexico City, the capital of Mexico, is today – on a lake. Huitzilopochtli, one of their gods, told them to build a city when they saw an eagle perched on a cactus, holding a snake. And when they did, on an island in the middle of a lake, they sailed over to it and started to build houses. When they ran out of space, they built more islands and linked them all together by bridges. They connected the islands to the mainland by causeways 'as wide as two cavalry lances', according to the Spaniards who were the first Europeans to go there.

'Did you go with the Spanish conquistadors, Ka?'

She didn't answer. She was still washing.

'You're as clean as an Aztec, you are.'

Aztecs were amazingly clean and so were their towns. Slaves cleaned the streets every day. Tenochtitlan was beautiful, except for the pyramid in the middle, which was disgusting, because the steps were covered with blood and flies. The cleverness and the cruelty of the Aztecs shocked Captain Cortes, the Spanish leader, though by all accounts he was just as cruel. Topher scrolled down to a picture of the pyramid, an artist's impression showing all the gore.

'Did you see that, Ka?'

She stopped washing for a moment. Then started licking again, energetically, as if she didn't want to hear any more or think about what he had said. What had she seen? He remembered all the stuff about human sacrifice and found a different picture, an artist's impression of Tenochtitlan, which made it look beautiful, like Venice, but with more trees. It seemed the Aztecs set trees in the mud at the bottom of the lake to anchor the floating islands. Interesting – till the battery ran out. He'd better recharge it in case Molly needed it.

The phone was ringing as he got in the house.

It was Ellie, his friend who lived in London. She

wanted to organise a half-term visit. Ellie was a great organiser, which was okay when you wanted something organising. A trip to London would be great, so he let her suggest dates and stuff and dutifully wrote it down.

'What've you been up to?' she said when he'd done all that.

'Not a lot.' He told her about moving the cats into the shed because of Tally's allergy. 'If it is an allergy.'

'It seems worth trying to find out.'

'Yes, but it's not fair to Ka. How's Duo by the way?'

Duo was one of Ka's kittens. She'd had four after their Roman trip.

'Great! He's so funny. He chases the football when there's a match on the telly.'

'Ka used to do that, but she can't now she's banished. She's been AWOL again, by the way.'

'AWOL?'

'Absent without leave.' It was good telling Clever Clogs Ellie something.

They talked about the cats for a bit, but he didn't mention the time-travelling. He'd tried once but she hadn't believed him. She wasn't keen on history either. She said people in the past were too cruel. Well, she was right about that. That's why he didn't want Ka to go there. But he did want to know about where she'd been.

He got onto the internet again later, on his own computer. What bird did that feather come from? It didn't take him long to find out. There were pictures of lots of colourful Mexican birds, but the most famous was the quetzal, a green-headed bird with a luminous red breast

25

and long emerald green tail feathers. He held the red feather against the screen. It matched exactly. He read: *The quetzal was one of the most revered creatures of the Aztec or Mexica tribe. Its iridescent feathers – green and red – formed the headdress of their chiefs.* There was a picture of Montezuma, their most famous chief, wearing one when he met Captain Cortes.

Later he went down to the shed to say goodnight to Ka. Tally had been crying on and off all evening, though there wasn't a cat hair in the house, so he felt sure cat hairs weren't the problem. Molly had said she thought Tally might be teething. As his feet crunched on the frosty grass he looked forward to telling Ka she might soon be allowed back in the house. But as soon as he switched on the torch, the beam fell on the empty basket and then the empty armchair. Buggins was in his box, but there was no sign of Ka. At first he wasn't worried. On a clear night like this Ka and Zingi were probably out hunting. But then he swept the torch round the shed and saw the statue, on its side, in the corner behind the door. His heart sank – till he saw it rocking. She was coming back to life!

He stood transfixed. 'Come on, Ka!'

He held his breath, but the transformation didn't follow. The rocking stopped. The statue went still again, as if Ka had given up, exhausted. Now he began to feel uneasy. The rocking, the *juddering* had looked desperate, as if she were fighting for her life. He switched off his torch to see if the stone glowed in the dark, and it didn't. Switching the torch on again, he picked up the statue and carried it inside, feeling certain that Ka was in danger.

The house was quiet. At least Tally had stopped crying. His dad was in the kitchen getting a glass. Something was wrong here too. The house felt eerily quiet. Without speaking his dad rushed out of the kitchen and headed for the stairs. Topher followed him. Standing on the landing he saw Molly leaning over Tally's cot.

'Give the glass to me.'

She pressed it against the skin on Tally's neck.

'Look, they don't go away.'

She lifted Tally out of her cot.

'W-what is it?' Topher hardly dare ask. Molly and his dad exchanged a quick fraught glance.

'Spots,' said Molly, 'not going away, when you press a glass against them, it's a bad sign.'

'Of what?'

She started wrapping bedclothes round Tally. 'We must get her to hospital.'

'Ambulance?' His dad got his mobile.

'I think we can get her there quicker. Car keys?'

They raced downstairs. Topher followed, but as his dad opened the front door he said, 'It's best if you stay here. Ring Casualty and tell them to be ready for us. Tell them we've a suspected case of meningitis. Then go to bed.'

He closed the door.

Meningitis! Topher remembered hearing about it on the news. It was a terrible disease. Tally could ... He didn't let himself think the thought.

The phone was by the door. He put the statue down and looked up the number with shaking hands.

'My little sister, my mum and dad are bringing her in. They think she's got meningitis. They should be there in about ten minutes. Get everything ready.' *Don't let her die.*

He picked up the statue and climbed the stairs, feeling sick with guilt. He'd wanted something else to be the matter with Tally, and it was. She wasn't allergic to cat hair, she was seriously ill. He felt as if he'd wished it upon her and as if he were shrinking with shame. *Live, Tally, live, and Ka, come back. I need you.*

He put the cold statue beside his bed. The moon flooded his room with light, but the stone still looked dull. He drew the curtains to see if he could detect a glow when it was dark, but he couldn't see anything. He opened the curtains, looked out on the star-filled night – and saw something else shining in the sky. An aeroplane? A comet? A UFO? Whatever it was, it seemed to be heading for the house. Getting closer and closer. Moving very fast – as it headed straight for him. It would crash into the house at this rate. He ducked – but then it seemed to be slowing down. It looked less like an aircraft, more like a bird. Yes a huge bird with a dipping flight was heading this way, over the trees at the bottom of the garden, over the shed. It reminded him of the woodpecker he sometimes saw in the garden, but this bird was bigger and brighter. Green and red flashed intermittently as long pointed wings flapped, then pulled back. It was slowing itself down. For a moment it seemed to be hanging in the air, but it was getting closer. Closer. Closer. Very close.

It landed on the edge of the conservatory roof. Now

he could see yellow talons gripping the guttering. Round enquiring eyes met his as it looked up at the window. Not a woodpecker, it was much bigger and the top of its head was a crest of green-gold feathers. Its body was green, but its breast was a bright metallic red which he'd seen before.

As the bird began to walk up the sloping roof, iridescent, emerald green tail feathers fanned out behind it, and Topher felt a sense of destiny. He wasn't surprised when it tapped on the window with a pointed yellow beak. He climbed onto the windowsill and opened the window. Then he stepped outside. He wasn't surprised that the roof held his weight. He knew that he'd shrunk because it had happened before, and he knew what to do next. He walked round to the bird's tail and climbed up the stiff feathers till he reached the top. Up went the tail tipping him onto its back in a kneeling position.

What happened next was a surprise. He expected the bird to turn round, walk to the edge of the sloping roof and then take off. But it started walking backwards. He had to cling to its neck to stop sliding off. Down down down it stepped – and off the edge! He braced himself for a fall, but then as the bird flapped its wings furiously, fanning his hair, it began to rise and seconds later it surged into the air! Higher and higher it flew. Below him shed, garden pond and trees appeared and disappeared in rapid succession and he knew he was beginning another journey through space and time.

Chapter 6

Up and down, up and down flapped the bird's wings. Whoosh! Whoosh!

As the Chichester streets passed beneath him, he looked for his parents' car. Had they reached the hospital yet? But the cars below looked like crawling ants, and buildings like Lego blocks. Whoosh! Whoosh! Up and down went the quetzal's wings and soon the town was behind them. Now they flew over forests and fields, a patchwork of green and brown. Up and down. Up and down. At first the bird's dipping flight felt like a roller coaster ride and he half-expected a sudden drop. But it kept climbing, blurring roads and buildings, land and sea, as it got faster and faster and smoother and smoother. Wing beats grew quieter and then . . . silence . . . for they were in space. And . . . stillness . . . for the bird was resting its wings but, amazingly, they were still whizzing past balls of fire, which were stars close-up, and balls of fire with tails, which were comets close-up! On his first trip he'd been terrified. Now it was thrilling as shooting stars and comets whizzed to and fro, criss-crossing the sky like a brilliant firework display! And what was that on his right-hand side? The Earth, he could see it again clearly, hanging in space, a globe of brilliant blue and green!

But not for long. As the bird zoomed deeper into space, faster than the speed of light, Earth grew smaller, smaller, smaller. Vanished. They'd left it behind. They'd left Earth's stratosphere – were zooming towards other galaxies – in order to re-enter at some other time. What had the great scientist Einstein said? If you travelled as far as the nearest star, when you came back to earth you would be younger than when you'd set off, *because you'd have travelled back in time*? Yes! And he, Topher Hope, had proved it three times. He'd been a priestess's son in Ancient Egypt. He'd been a mosaic-maker's apprentice in Roman Britain. In Tudor times he'd helped a magician search for the philosopher's stone. So where was he going now and who would he be?

He had a hunch. Just hoped he'd get there in time to save Ka.

In time. Out of time. Through time.

Faster and faster he flew.

Stars surrounded him. He must have passed thousands already, and there were thousands more ahead. So how far back had he travelled and when would he arrive? He willed his thoughts to Ka.

Hang on! I'm coming!

Hang on! I'm coming!

She was in danger. He was sure of it. She needed him.

I must get there in time.

That was his last thought as he rested his head on the bird's neck, and found the feathers surprisingly soft and springy. Closing his eyes for a moment he felt his head nodding. Then he must have fallen asleep, for when he opened his eyes, he could see Earth ahead of him.

He had left Earth and he was coming back to Earth, which

looked like a blue ball. The sea was deep blue and the land-masses were an even deeper blue. Then other colours came into view, landmasses of green and brown and white. For now the quetzal was *zooming* towards Earth. It was getting closer and closer by the second. There were the Americas, north and south, both very green with a narrow neck of land between them.

Whoosh! Whoosh!

The quetzal's wings started to beat again. The bird was heading for that narrow neck of land. It was heading for Mexico! Blue-green sea on either side. Bright red beaches. Vivid green jungle. Volcanoes belching fire. A black mountain rising to meet them. Oh no, they were going to crash into the mountain! But the bird veered to one side. Clever bird! He clung onto its neck, afraid of sliding, afraid of lurching over its head, afraid of hurtling into rocks below. But the bird was skirting the mountain, skirting the jungle on the lower slopes, and seemed to know what it was doing. Dark crags loomed on one side, the frothing sea on the other – and between them was a narrow belt of red beach. Could it land there? Topher closed his eyes and kept them closed as it began its descent. Opened them. He was in the past. For a few seconds he knew that, though he couldn't see much for the air was filled with smoke. What was that bird flying away? Why was the wooden floor beneath his feet moving and why was he wearing tights? And where was Ka? Ka! That's why he was here! That much he remembered as all memory of his future self faded and he became Topher Esperanza, cabin boy to the famous Spanish explorer, Captain Hernan Cortes.

Chapter 7

He was on the deck of a burning ship!

The bows to his right were smouldering.

'Ka! Ka!' Topher called her name as he searched the deck, keeping his head down, so that Captain Cortes couldn't see him. He would be furious if he knew his cabin boy was still aboard the *San Antonio*, searching for the ship's cat. The air round him was filled with smoke. Smoke billowed into the sky and flames leaped to reach them. He hadn't got much time. In the sea round him more Spanish galleons burned. Others were half under water, deliberately scuttled to make them sink – on Cortes' orders, to stop faint-hearted conquistadors from sailing back to Spain or Cuba. Now sparks burst into the air. A wind had got up. The bows flared. Burning oak cracked.

'Ka! Ka!'

Where now? He'd searched the galley. He'd searched his own bunk. He'd searched all her favourite places, including the captain's luxurious cabin, now stripped of its luxuries. Cushions, curtains and tapestries now adorned Cortes' mansion in Veracruz. As the wind blew some smoke away, Topher glimpsed the town – and the towers of Cortes' mansion – and his master, on the beach on his dark chestnut stallion.

'No going back!' The wind carried some of his words to the burning ship.

'Stay! . . . in land of Mexico – conquer!'

To Topher his words were like bullets. Never to see his family again! Never to leave this land! All the more reason to find Ka.

'Ka! Ka! Puss, puss, puss!'

She could have moved, that was the trouble, might be somewhere he'd already looked.

As he searched the cabin again, he remembered how, back in Spain, he'd joined the *San Antonio* to become the great explorer's cabin boy. He'd wanted adventure – in the Indies, as men called the western isles – and sailing to the island of Cuba had been an adventure, but this trip to the unknown mainland was looking like an adventure too many. And it wouldn't have happened if Cortes had stayed in Cuba, if he hadn't fought with the Governor who had called him traitor. Cortes said he wanted to defeat the Aztecs who ruled the land and make them faithful subjects of the King of Spain. The Governor said Cortes wanted to sail to the mainland and make himself King – and now some conquistadors thought the Governor was right. That's why they wanted to sail back to Cuba.

'Ka! Ka!' Topher came out onto the deck again.

Where could she be? Why hadn't she kept close to him when they were ordered to leave the ship? They could have gone ashore together.

He was beginning to wonder if she had already gone, by herself, when he heard a cry.

'Mwaa!' He scanned the deck.

'Where are you, Ka?'

'Mwaa!' Where *was* she?

'Mwaa! Mwaa!' Then he realised the cry was coming from above. And there she was in the rigging! In the crow's-nest near the top of the mainmast!

Not clever, Ka. 'Come down!'

'Mwaa- aa!' *Can't! Can't!*

''Course you can, you've done it before!'

He'd seen her racing up and down the rigging. Sometimes they both went up to the crow's-nest for a bit of peace and quiet.

'Mwaa – ow! Mwaa – ow!' *Can't now! Can't now!*

'Why not?' But even as he spoke he knew he was going to have to climb up and see for himself. But could he do it without being seen? Luckily the crowd on shore seemed focused on another blazing ship. There was a roar as a mainsail went up in a sheet of flame. Perhaps if he climbed the rigging on the other side, the mast would hide him and no one would see him?

He started to climb.

At least Ka stayed quiet. She knew he was coming to rescue her. But why had she climbed up there? She was usually such a sensible cat. And why didn't she climb down now to meet him?

'Ka! Start climbing down!'

'Mwaa!' *Can't!*

He climbed as fast as he could but had to keep stopping to wipe flakes of burning debris from his eyes. And now he could feel the heat from the *Santa Maria* next to the *San Antonio*. Its mainmast was a column of fire.

He looked down briefly. It made him feel sick. Flames

35

had crept about a quarter of the way up the deck. Not too bad. They were moving slowly. The wind had dropped. He scanned the shore. Had anyone noticed him? Not Cortes anyway. He was riding away from the beach. All other eyes were on the blazing ships – except for one man's, except for Pedro de Alvarado, the second in command. Topher recognised the pale yellow hair which gave him his nickname El Sol, The Sun. There was no hiding in a crowd with hair like that, not among the conquistadors. A few were fair like Topher himself, but most were dark haired, and so were the Indians, though their heavy black hair was straight and long, except for the warriors in their topknots. But it wasn't just El Sol's hair which distinguished him from the rest of the crowd. It was the telescope he held to his eye.

Now Topher felt El Sol's steely eyes on him as he climbed. Why was he so interested? He didn't like Ka. He called her *bruja* or witch. Luckily Cortes did like her because she'd kept the *San Antonio* free of rats, so El Sol dared not harm her. *Dared* not – while Cortes was aboard, and not while they needed Ka. But now? Topher climbed faster, suddenly full of suspicion.

A shout went up. People had seen him. El Sol must have told them there was sport to be had. Now noise surrounded him – the roar of the sea, the crack of burning wood, and the shouts of a crowd.

'Topher! Topher!' He could just make out what they were shouting.

'Topher! Topher!' It became clearer and faster.

'Topher! Topher!' It was a chant; they were cheering

36

him on as if he were climbing the greasy pole at a fiesta. Now all eyes were on him. Five hundred Spaniards cheered. No, not that many now. Several had died of jungle fever or been killed by Indians. Indians watched too, hundreds of them. Some were friendly like the Totonacs, who hated being part of the Aztec empire and wanted to help Cortes overthrow it. Others had been cowed by the sight of the two-headed, six-legged warriors. That's what they thought men on horseback were, because they'd never seen horses before, or big ships, or cannon, or the guns called arquebuses, which they called 'lightning sticks'.

'Mwa!'

'Nearly there, Ka.'

Why didn't she come down to meet him? Then he reached the top and saw why. She was *tied* to the top of the mast. A cheer went up, then it went quiet. Was El Sol boasting about what he had done?

'Mwaa!'

'I'm being as quick as I can, Ka.' He felt for the knife in his belt. Then as fast and as carefully as he could, he cut though the cord binding her body to the mast. She dropped into his hands, too weak to move. The marks of the cord were still in her fur, in her skin most likely. There was no time to look.

What now? Could she climb down?

He glanced below. The fire was halfway across the deck, about three yards from the mast. They must get down quickly. Get off the boat.

Ka was still, as if life had been squeezed out of her.

'I'll carry you. But you mustn't . . . ' He'd been going to say 'dig your claws in', but saw there was no need. She had no claws left. There was no fur on her belly and there was blood on her mouth. He slipped her inside his shirt. Then he started to climb downwards, Ka thumping – gently he hoped – against his stomach, held firm by his belt.

No one cheered.

The mood had changed.

Glancing down he saw why.

He felt sick, sicker than usual.

Flames were licking round the base of the mast.

A wind had got up again. Flames were leaping across the deck. The bridge was a roaring furnace. He speeded up. Got within three yards of the base, could feel the heat, see the rising flames. Was he going to be burned alive?

'Sorry, Ka, but I've got to jump.'

He must leap as far from the mast as he could, make a run for it over the burning deck, then climb up and over the side into the sea where he could wade ashore.

He jumped. He ran. He climbed onto the side. But there below him was the sea, deeper than when he'd waded aboard. The tide had come in. He couldn't wade now. He'd have to swim to shore – on his back, or Ka would drown – hoping no waves went over his head. Carefully, he started to ease himself – and Ka – over the side.

'TOPHER!'

Looking up, he saw a small rowing boat.

Bartolomé! Topher recognised the Dominican friar pulling the oars. The cowl of his black cloak had slipped, exposing his tonsured head.

38

Bartolomé was rowing furiously but it seemed ages before he reached the *San Antonio*.

'You will have to jump down, Topher. I will keep the craft as steady as I can.'

Topher jumped.

Thanks be to God for Bartolomé de las Casas, the kindest and most just of men! No wonder the King of Spain had made him Protector of the Indians, for he was kind to all men. Now he was pulling hard on an oar, turning the boat round. 'How's Ka? As soon as...I heard what...El Sol had...done...' Bartolomé didn't finish. He was too busy trying to row the boat.

Ka's eyes shone from the darkness.

'I think she'll be all right.'

'When we get...back to shore...I have some... ointments. How are you?'

'Fine.' Topher answered automatically, but when they got to the shore, and he tried to get out of the boat, he couldn't. The soles of his feet were raw.

Bartolomé lifted him out of the boat. Others came to help, even El Sol, who steadied the boat with a sardonic grin. 'So, you saved the life of the little witch, did you? Then you are even cleverer than Bartolomé here. He didn't manage to stop us burning the Indians on Cuba.'

'But he has saved many others, Pedro,' said Francisco, another friar, taking Topher from Bartolomé's arms. 'And King Carlos himself said it was an unchristian act. He has forbidden the killing of Indians as if they were beasts.'

'But King Carlos isn't here, is he, holy man?' El Sol

39

had seen Cortes riding up and raised his voice. 'Governor General Cortes gives the orders here.'

Cortes dismounted, looking every inch the conquistador in doublet and hose and plumed hat. 'What is wrong with my little cabin boy?'

'He has blistered feet, rope burns on his hands and smoke in his lungs,' said Bartolomé.

'Because he disobeyed your orders,' said El Sol. 'He stayed on the burning ship.'

'To look for Ka.' Topher struggled from Francisco's arms, flinching as his feet touched the sand, but he was determined to stand up for himself and show respect to his master.

'You risked your life for the *cat*?' Cortes stroked his beard and shook his head. 'Is Ka worth such devotion?'

'I think she is – and...' Topher stopped. Ka was moving. He felt her climbing up his chest, saw her head stick out.

'Mwa!'

Cortes noticed the blood on her mouth. 'Is she injured?'

'Yes, because El Sol tied her to the top of the mast.'

'Is this true?' Cortes turned to his second in command. 'Couldn't you find enough Indians to torture?'

El Sol shrugged. 'No ships, no need for a ship's cat.'

Cortes handed El Sol the reins of his horse.

'I trust you can stable Diablo without harming him? Rub him down. Check his hooves. He has ridden over rough ground today. And tell the guards to open the town gates, for it will soon be nightfall and everyone should get back inside.'

Topher saw El Sol redden to the roots of his pale yellow hair, because Cortes was treating him like a humble groom and messenger boy. As he led Diablo away, his steely blue eyes bored into Topher. Unspoken words hung in the air. *I'll get you for this.* Topher's feet burned and his head throbbed. He knew that El Sol had never been his friend. He knew he hated Ka. Now he knew they both had a dangerous enemy.

Chapter 8

Bartolomé and Francisco made a seat with their hands and carried Topher between them so his feet swung free. As they walked up the beach towards the town gates they heard Cortes, behind them, shouting orders, and his interpreter, Jeronimo, translating them into Mayan.

'Gentlemen, hurry inside the town! And tell the Indians!'

Jeronimo had been a prisoner of the Mayan tribe for two years till Cortes had rescued him. There were many dangers in these parts. Night, which fell swiftly, added to them, though attacks could come at any time. And attacks were expected, from Montezuma, chief of the Aztecs, who claimed he was ruler of the whole of this land, though he lived far away on the other side of the mountains. But he had spies everywhere and his warriors could attack by land, sea or river. So the town called Veracruz was a garrison, surrounded by a stockade.

Cortes caught up with Bartolomé and Francisco just before they reached the gates, and spoke to them like old friends.

'While you were enjoying the bonfires I rode towards the mountains to see if they're made of gold, as some say.' He laughed. 'But if they are, their gods are keeping it well hidden by jungle.'

'Not their gods, Captain Cortes, our God,' said Bartolomé.

Cortes crossed himself, and as the gates swung open he shouted up to the Spanish guards, 'I'm glad to see you're still there. I thought everyone had gone to see the bonfires!'

A wide street lined with buildings led straight to a small wooden church, for a town in the Spanish style had replaced the Totonac village the conquistadors found when they arrived. The street was empty today – everyone had gone to the beach – and it wasn't long before they reached the town square. Church, town hall and a court of justice with a prison filled three sides, and Cortes' own mansion filled the fourth. He stopped under its arched entrance.

'Is it not beautiful, a real home from home!' He pointed to his coat of arms carved above the doorway. 'We can be rich and happy in New Spain, can we not?'

'We can be happy anywhere – God willing,' said Bartolomé.

Cortes crossed himself again as the door opened and his chamberlain welcomed him home with a sweeping bow.

A huge tree arched over the house, a tree sacred to the Indians, and Topher remembered their gasps when Cortes cut into its buttressed trunk. Three times he'd struck it, saying, 'I take possession of this tree in the name of the Father, the Son and the Holy Ghost!' Then he'd taken a spade and started to dig the foundations of his house, calling on all the conquistadors to build houses for themselves too. On that day the tree had been covered with pink and white flowers. Now long pods hung from its branches, and he could see why the Indians called it Smoking Tree. The pods were bursting open and white fibres were floating upwards in fluffy clouds. Watching them, Topher saw an Indian woman standing silently on the balcony above. She wore a red cape and her black hair was tied on the top of her head in two bunches like a cow's horns. She was an Aztec, who had thrown in her lot with the Spanish, but Cortes called her Doña Marina or wife, though he had a Spanish wife back in Cuba.

Cortes saw her too and turned to Bartolomé. 'Take Topher back to your house and make him and Ka well again – as quickly as you can. I want boy and cat back quickly. No one polishes my sword as well as Topher, and we have rats and mice for Ka just like in the old country.'

He went inside and they heard him telling the chamberlain to tell Doña Isabella about Topher. She was one of a few Spanish women who had come with the conquistadors to look after the sick and wounded.

As Bartolomé and Francisco set off across the square, Topher looked back and saw Cortes on the balcony kissing Doña Marina on the lips.

'We have rats and mice because we brought them here,' said Francisco.

'Along with many bad things,' said Bartolomé. 'Doña Isabella has too many sick and wounded to care for.'

But a shout interrupted them. 'Stop!' Cortes was leaning over the balcony. 'Doña Marina wants to see the cat!'

As the friars headed back, Topher remembered how Doña Marina called Ka 'little *ocelotl*' when she first saw her. In Nahuatl, the Aztec language, *ocelotl* meant jaguar. It was the name of one of their gods and of their fiercest warriors. He loosened his shirt as Doña Marina came out of the door.

'Hello, little *ocelotl*. But oh...' She saw Ka's raw skin and called up to Cortes, 'That El Sol is a brute!'

'I think he has learned his lesson.'

'I hope so. Aztec people, they think Ka just like god Ocelotl and punish men who do dishonour...'

'Many did see him,' said Francisco.

'Then he must look to his back,' said Doña Marina, straightening to her full height. She was taller than most Indians. Rings of green jade swung from her ears, but unlike most Aztecs her brown face was smooth, not studded with colourful stones.

Bartolomé and Francisco carried Topher back to their house behind the church. The church was built from wood in the Spanish fashion with a bell-tower, but as yet no bell. The friars' house was a simpler building, built of mud-bricks with rounded corners and a thatched roof. It was like the dwellings they had found when they arrived in Veracruz, with bright red trumpet-like flowers growing round the doorway. Inside was cool and dark and comfortable. Francisco lit an oil lamp. Bartolomé sat Topher on a bed near the back wall. 'Rest there for a while.'

Francisco brought him a drink of something sweet.

Bartolomé returned with a bowl of water. Then he knelt and bathed Topher's feet.

'Now let's get you into a clean shirt.'

'But Ka...'

'We'll take care of her too.' Gently Francisco undid Topher's shirt and Bartolomé took Ka into his arms. Topher lay down, and as the pain began to ebb, he felt sleepy. There was a stillness about Bartolomé, even when he was moving, that made you feel calm. He was cleaning Ka's wounds now and she was purring. *Rrrr...est. Rrrr...est. Rrr...est.*

When he woke he could hear the murmur of voices. It was morning. He could feel the sun even before he opened his eyes. It was streaming through the door lighting the backs of two shaved heads. Plump Francisco and lean Bartolomé were at separate tables writing. He could hear their quill pens scratching the parchment. For a few moments he was confused. Why wasn't he on the floor outside Cortes' door, waiting for him to call for food or drink? Then he remembered what had happened and lifted the coverlet. How was Ka? He could feel her against his stomach, soft and warm, not stiff and tense, so he felt hopeful. He touched her ears and her eyes shone from the darkness. Amber circles. She blinked, seemed content. He didn't speak because he wanted to enjoy the moment, and when she began to purr, he closed his eyes and let the coverlet fall.

Later, the men began to talk in low voices and he couldn't help listening, even when he realised they were talking about things they would prefer him not to hear – like Doña Marina and Cortes. Francisco was worried about their mortal souls.

'Cortes is committing adultery. It is against the commandments. He is living with a woman who is not his wife.'

'Yes, it is a grave sin, but...' Bartolomé spoke slowly as if thinking about every word, 'she has become a Christian – Father Sahagun baptised her – and she may prevent Cortes from committing worse sins, like killing more Indians.'

'How will she do that?'

'Because she is an Indian.'

'But the other Indians despise her as a traitor! She has renounced their gods. She has embraced all things Spanish, including our Governor.'

Cortes had just had himself made Governor General of Veracruz, by the town council of Veracruz, which he had appointed. He said he was equal to the Governor of Cuba now, and answerable only to the King of Spain.

Bartolomé went on. 'She speaks two of their languages, even better than Jeronimo. With her Cortes can conquer with words not swords, win hearts and minds for Christ. And not all Indians despise her. Her noble birth, her proud bearing commands respect. Don't forget she was the daughter of an Aztec noble.'

Topher had heard that before. Doña Marina had lived like an Aztec princess till her father died. But then her mother married again and gave her away to a passing trader. The trader sold her as a slave to a Tabasco chief. Then the chief gave her to Cortes with twenty other women, but he had kept her for himself, because she was so clever and beautiful.

'She will help Cortes win this land for Christ,'

Bartolomé went on. 'She speaks Nahuatl, the language of her people the Aztecs, and Mayan, the language of the Yucatan, and she is quickly learning Spanish. She can tell many tribes about Christianity. She can explain that we come in peace and mean no harm.'

'If only that were true . . . ' The fat friar shook his head.

'We must make it true. We must persuade Cortes that peace and persuasion are better than blood and fire. He is starting to see that. He is a Christian. He knows that the Totonacs are our allies because we treat them with Christian kindness. The Aztecs take their food and sacrifice their children. We protect them and gain nothing by killing them.'

'Except their land?'

'Which they kill us for taking.'

'Unless we kill them first, as we did in Cuba.'

'But we lost their souls – and probably our own as well – for we destroyed a whole people.'

'The Governor of Cuba and many others say Indians are not people, but animals.'

Bartolomé buried his face in his hands. 'Cortes cannot say these people are animals and live with one of them as his wife. Perhaps, with all his faults he is a better man than the Governor of Cuba.'

Topher heard more voices outside and saw a ball fly past the doorway. A Totonac boy ran by and then another, two of a gang of boys racing past on their way to the ball court. Three boys stopped and stood in the doorway and stared in. And Topher stared back – he couldn't help it –

48

they looked so strange with their long black hair and stones studding their bottom lips. Topher knew one of the boys quite well. He called him Nico. It sounded a bit like his real name, which was very long and was actually a number, the date on which he was born.

'Bartolomé, how is Topher?' Nico asked in Nahuatl, as the other boys strained to see inside the white men's house. They didn't have tables and chairs and beds in their own dwellings. 'The white chief says he needs medicine and stays with you.'

Bartolomé glanced at Topher, saw that he was awake and walked over. 'He is not too bad,' he replied also in Nahuatl, as he laid a hand on Topher's forehead. 'And as soon as his feet heal he'll play with you again. But he rests now. Come and see him tomorrow.'

The boy waved at Topher, then shouted, '*Adios, amigo!*' and ran off with the others.

Bartolomé laughed. 'Did you understand that? His Nahuatl, I mean, not his Spanish?'

'Yes.' Topher felt pleased with himself. He had been trying hard to learn the local language.

Bartolomé examined Topher's feet.

'They have begun to heal already. In a few days you will be running errands for Cortes.'

'And playing *tlachtli*.'

'You'll have to be very fit for that crazy game.'

Crazy was the word. You had to hit the hard rubber ball with your knees, hips and elbows, bounce it off the four walls of the ball court. Two teams competed against each other very fiercely.

'Drink this to build up your strength,' said Francisco. 'The Aztecs call it xocolatl or Food of the Gods. I have sweetened it with honey. Good? Yes?'

'Very good,' Topher agreed after a couple of sips. It was the same drink he'd had the night before.

'How can anyone say Indians are not human when they have invented a drink like this – from beans?' said Francisco. 'And it would be even better made with milk. When we go to Spain, we will bring back a cow. Then we will have butter and cheese for our bread.'

'And milk for Ka.' Topher peeped at her under the covers. 'But how will you get back to Spain without a ship?'

'Don't worry about that.' Bartolomé smiled, so that his eyes crinkled at the edges. 'Cortes is not stupid. He burnt some boats but not all of them, and those he sunk lie on their sides quite near the shore. The holes in their sides can be mended, and will be if he wishes.'

'But does he wish to return to Spain?'

Bartolemé shrugged. 'Perhaps you'll find out when you return to his service.'

Ka was stirring. She'd heard the word of her favourite drink.

'Sorry, Ka, no milk today. Try this.' Topher dipped his finger in the chocolate drink and she licked it clean with a few flicks of her rough tongue.

'I'll get her fresh water and turkey meat,' said Francisco, who loved cooking.

Bartolomé knelt and gently examined Ka's paws and furless belly.

'She too is healing. Don't be sad, Topher. It is not so bad here and it could be Paradise. Sometimes it makes me think of the Garden of Eden, there are so many beautiful things. Look.' He pointed to the doorway, where a brilliant coloured bird seemed to hang in the air by a bright red trumpet flower. 'Can you hear its wings humming? If we all live as true Christians and show the Indians that our God is kind, they will become Christians too. Then we can all live in peace and plenty. I am hopeful that at their next festival, the Aztec priests will let them sacrifice an image made of dough instead of a girl.'

'I hope so,' said Topher, 'because if not Nico's sister will die.'

Nico hadn't seen his sister for a year, since she was chosen to be the wife of the Maize God. He would see her on the day of the festival, but never again if the sacrifice went ahead in the old way.

Later, as he fed Ka with tiny pieces of turkey meat, Topher wished he could stay for ever with Bartolomé and Francisco, their little house was so peaceful. But in a week his feet were better and he had to return to the hurly-burly of his master's mansion where you never knew what might happen.

'Topher! Ka! Both on your feet I see!' Cortes did seem pleased to see them as he hurried out of the front door. He stopped for a moment to stroke Ka, and issue orders to Topher.

'First, get yourself to the armour room and clean my sword, the one there, not this one.' He patted the hilt and chuckled. 'I'm off to the courthouse and may need to chop off a few heads today.'

Topher's heart sank when he reached the armoury at the back of the house. What a mess! It looked as if no one had been in there all week. Or perhaps someone had, for the sand bucket was empty, and he was sure he'd left it full. But the armour on the table in the middle looked rustier than ever. The damp sea air had done its worst. He'd better get to work. When Cortes went into battle he had to be covered with steel from head to toe. It would take days to scour it, but first he must fetch more sand.

He grabbed the bucket. 'Are you coming to the beach, Ka, or staying there?'

Her answer was a purr as she lay curled up in Cortes' leather-lined helmet.

As he searched the beach for sharp dry sand he recalled the beach in Cuba, where the Spanish had tied an Indian chief to a stake and burned him. He remembered Bartolomé pleading with him to become a Christian, so he would go to Heaven. The Indian said, 'Will I meet more Christians in your Heaven?' And when Bartolomé said he would the Indian replied, 'Then I will not be a Christian, for I would not go to a place where men are so cruel.'

For the Spanish had killed all his people, every single one. But here it was different. For a month now it had been peaceful. Bartolomé was right. Indians and Spaniards were both human and could live together in peace and plenty. With his bucket full, he turned to go back to the town, but something stopped him, a sudden

movement above the town. A strange bird he thought –
a turkey perhaps – was coming out of the jungle. But the
bird was bigger and more brightly coloured than a
turkey and there were more following it. But not birds.
Oh no! *People* were coming out of the jungle and they
weren't Spanish. Indians! They might even be Aztecs!
And more and more of them were coming out of the
jungle. Dropping the bucket, he began to run. This could
be an attack! He must warn the guards, if he could reach
the gates before they did!

Chapter 9

Breathless, he did reach the gates before the strangers and a guard pulled him inside. 'Yes, don't worry. We've seen them!'

Cortes arrived moments later, with El Sol and Jeronimo. Foot soldiers followed with pikes and lances. Archers scrambled up to the battlements.

El Sol said, 'Shall I go wring the chief bird's neck before it causes trouble?'

Cortes said, 'Let's try talk first. But alert the cavalry in case it doesn't work.'

El Sol left for the stables as Cortes and Jeronimo climbed the watchtower. Topher followed – in case his master needed a message taking – but as he reached the top of the steps, Cortes grabbed him. 'Look at this pantomime, Topher.' He lifted him onto his shoulders. 'I don't think we've much to be afraid of, do you?'

Topher laughed. There were about twenty men in loincloths and short cloth capes, led by another covered in brightly coloured feathers.

'A parrot! Can he talk?' said Cortes. 'Ask him who he is and whence he comes.'

Jeronimo addressed the man in Nahuatl.

And the man replied in Nahuatl, loudly and with much waving of his arms. Topher understood some of it, but was glad of Jeronimo's translation.

'He says his name is Teudile. He is the chief steward of Montezuma, King of the Aztecs, who lives on the other side of yonder mountain. He brings greetings from his king and gifts.'

Each of the followers carried a large sack or bundle.

'Tell him to hand over the gifts,' said Cortes.

Jeronimo translated and the Indian replied, 'A foreign vassal does not give orders to the steward of a great king.'

Cortes looked amused. 'Tell him who I am, Jeronimo, and warn him he'd better do as I say.'

Jeronimo replied, but more politely, Topher thought.

'My lord requests that you hand over the gifts your master has so generously sent to his master, King Carlos of Spain, who rules the greater part of the world.'

At this Teudile licked his finger, touched the sandy ground and raised it to his lips. He was symbolically eating dirt, Jeronimo explained, and it was a mark of great respect.

'Good,' said Cortes. 'Your words seem to have done the trick.'

Now Teudile beckoned one of his followers who stepped forward with a large sack. Then he asked for the gates to be opened.

'Tell them to open the sack there,' said Cortes. 'There may be an assassin inside.'

Jeronimo said, 'It doesn't look heavy enough for that.'

'Get it opened anyway.'

Jeronimo passed on the order, but once again phrased it, Topher thought, more diplomatically.

Even so, Teudile was offended.

Jeronimo turned to Cortes. 'He says that an ambassador of the King of all the Aztecs should be received inside your city walls, not outside like a beggar.'

Cortes laughed. 'Well, I think there are enough of us to deal with them even if they do want a fight. Give me time to get back to my house then open the gates. Keep a close watch, mind you. There may be more of them hiding in the jungle. Check that this lot are not armed. Then bring them to my throne room. If they want a pantomime they shall have it. Come on, Topher, there's work to do!'

Throne room? Pantomime? What was Cortes talking about?

The work was rearranging the furniture in Cortes' grandest room, which had many carved beams hung with rich tapestries. As he ordered servants to place his most ornate chair like a throne, on a dais at the end of the room, Doña Marina appeared, dressed like a Spanish lady in a full-skirted, tightly-bodiced dress. But when Cortes told her what was happening she looked concerned.

'From Montezuma you say? Then you must be cautious, my lord. Do not be deceived by the benign appearance of his steward. The Aztecs are the most ruthless and warlike of all tribes. Their warriors are thirsty for blood. They will stop at nothing to bring all peoples under his rule.'

Cortes gave orders for guards to be doubled. Then he sent Topher to fetch Bartolomé and Francisco from the church. 'And as many priests and friars as you can find. We shall need God on our side!'

Teudile and his followers, still carrying their bundles,

were entering the square, as Topher came out of the church with the friars. His headdress swayed from side to side as he nodded graciously to a few Totonac onlookers. Topher ran ahead to tell Cortes the friars were coming, and found an armed guard of honour at the door. Cortes was at the far end of the room, on his 'throne' beneath a banner bearing the coat of arms of the King of Spain. He seemed to be enjoying himself, but his voice was urgent.

'Topher, get Ka! Quick! We need her.'

Luckily she was still in the armoury asleep in Cortes' helmet.

'Here,' said Cortes, pointing to the space between his knees, when Topher brought her in.

'Brothers, stand behind me!' he ordered Bartolomé and the other friars when they came in. 'We form an impressive sight, do we not?' He stroked Ka's ear. 'Doña Marina thinks they will be impressed to see the god Ocelotl residing with us. And you, Topher, kneel here.' Cortes pointed to his own feet. 'And make sure Ka does my bidding.'

She's a cat not a dog or a jaguar. Topher recalled seeing a real jaguar once on the edge of the jungle, but a fanfare of trumpets interrupted his thoughts. Teudile had arrived. The guard of honour raised their swords and lances to form an arch as he entered, and Doña Marina stepped forward to greet them in Nahuatl.

'You are welcome to the court of this great lord, who brings greetings from his king to yours. My lord asks if your lord is well?'

'My lord was well when I left. I trust the gods are still taking care of him.'

But Teudile didn't seem impressed by what he saw. He glanced scornfully at the carved wooden beams and richly embroidered wall hangings, and didn't seem to notice Ka.

Doña Marina prompted. 'My lord says you may present your lord's gifts.'

But Teudile looked huffy and said, 'I must discover my lord's wishes.'

Doña Marina advised him to hand over the gifts. He replied that he did not think her lord was worthy of the gifts. She advised him to be careful what he said, but he did not heed her warning. 'The great King Montezuma lives in a palace much more magnificent than this.' He tossed his head at the guard of honour. 'And his armies, lined up, would cover yours like the waves of the sea.'

'What is he saying?' Cortes was growing impatient. This was not going to plan.

Doña Marina told him and Cortes got to his feet.

'I think we must show this parrot how powerful we are. He will see we do not need huge armies. Topher, take Ka.'

Topher took Ka from the helmet and held her close. He guessed what was going to happen. As he stroked Ka's head he caught sight of Teudile noticing her. Did a glimmer of doubt cross his face? It was hard to say, so many ornaments distorted his features. Cortes put on his helmet and swept from the room. 'Follow me to the beach!'

Topher hoped Cortes didn't expect him to follow, not immediately. The beach would be no place for Ka. Even back here the noise would be scary. He must find somewhere safe for her.

'Come on, puss.' He carried her back to the armoury and closed doors and shutters to keep out as much sound as possible.

'Sorry, Ka. Try to sleep. I'll be back as soon as I can.'

He made his way to the beach as fast as he could. As he reached the top of the sand dunes, he could see nine cannon, lined up opposite a copse of palm trees. Men were ramming powder and shot into the barrels. Behind the cannon, on the edge of the sea, was a crowd including Teudile and the bearers – and Cortes. Further along the beach were the cavalry, eighteen men on horseback. Suddenly, at a word from Cortes, three of them charged – El Sol and his brothers, Topher thought. Blue eyes flashed behind visors as, swords waving and muskets firing, they galloped past the cannon, past Cortes and past the Indians who *quaked*. Topher, closer now, saw the fear in their faces, knew they had never seen horses before or muskets fired by gunpowder. And before they had time to recover from the shock, Cortes shouted, 'Big guns!'

There was a flurry of activity behind the cannon. A soldier rammed a smouldering rag into a barrel. Then – THUNDER! – a cannon ball hurtled through the air, shattering three palm trees into splinters. Teudile and the bearers fell backwards into the sea.

Back at Cortes' house, Teudile, feathers dripping, was still trembling, as he bade his bearers hand over the gifts. Topher, sitting at Cortes' feet, saw the bearers' hands shake as they untied their bundles.

'Feathers!' It was Cortes' turn to be scornful as parrot feathers, red, yellow and green, floated upwards.

'Beans!' His breath blasted the feathers higher.

'C-cocoa beans,' stammered Teudile. 'One hundred can b-buy you a slave.'

'When I want slaves I won't buy them,' Cortes replied.

There were other gifts, including precious stones, but only one brought a smile to Cortes' face, a mask of solid gold. Weighing it in his hand, he said, 'Sadly, my men suffer from a disease of the heart only curable by gold. I trust there is more where this came from?'

Teudile nodded and Cortes leaned towards Doña Marina, holding the mask in front of their faces. For a few moments the only sound in the room was their whispers. Then Cortes lowered the mask and addressed Teudile.

'Go tell your master that you have sorely offended me, for you failed to recognise your white-faced visitor from across the sea, or the god Ocelotl when he was here before you. Tell your master that two great gods bid him lay down his arms and prepare to worship a greater god, who is coming from the east to visit him.'

What did he mean?

Teudile seemed to understand for his mouth fell open and then he fainted.

Chapter 10

Next morning, as he searched for the bucket he'd left on the beach, Topher's mind was still full of questions. What had Doña Marina whispered to Cortes? What did he mean when he said 'a greater god' was going to visit Montezuma? When would they leave Veracruz? Nico appeared as he found the bucket, half hidden in the red sand.

'Topher, I come to invite you to our festival, the blessing of the maize seed.' The boy looked cheerful despite the turquoise weighing down his bottom lip.

'Sorry, Nico. I have too much work to do.'

'Not today. Tomorrow. Brother Bartolomé and Brother Francisco are coming – and we are not going to kill my sister.'

'Really?' That was good news.

'Yes. Truly. For whole week Brother Francisco help us make image from maize dough. It dry in sun and we sacrifice that instead. Brothers say the gods will be happy if we offer image of maiden.'

'I'm sure they will – and your sister?' Her name or number was long and complicated but began with P. 'I bet she's pleased too.'

'No.' Nico shook his head. 'Well, I not know because I haven't seen her for year. But my mother and father are worried. For whole year they prepare for this honour. For whole year my sister – she live like goddess. She ready to die and join the gods. Now they fear gods will be angry.'

'What does Bartolomé say about that?'

'He go see my parents and Aztec priests. He tell them of Christian god, more powerful than Aztec god, who make crops grow good. Well, we see if crops grow. That is why we have festival – to ask god to bless seed and make crops grow. Aztec priests say we sacrifice dough-god this year and see what happens.'

Topher sent up a prayer for better crops than usual. 'Where is the festival?'

'On temple pyramid, behind Christian church.'

'I shall come if I can, but I have to help my master get ready for journey to Tenochtitlan.'

'I know. I come too. And brothers. To fight Aztecs. Totonacs help Cortes overthrow tyrant Montezuma.'

Topher filled the bucket. So Cortes was planning to fight the Aztecs? That's why he wanted his armour clean.

'One more thing,' said Nico. 'After Maize Festival we play tlachtli to celebrate. You will, if gods allow, meet – how you say? – Patti.' There was a sparkle in Nico's dark brown eyes. He seemed happy that his sister was going to live. Topher remembered him saying that she was clever and beautiful. She was good at everything, even the ballgame, or had been till her parents stopped her playing with the boys. The priests chose the best to be sacrificed.

Later, Topher heard Cortes in the room next to the armoury.

'See this map, gentlemen? It shows our route to

Tenochtitlan. The journey should take sixty days. It is not the shortest route but it avoids tribes who may be hostile to us. This way we meet only tribes who hate and fear the Aztecs. They will help us by giving us supplies and men to help us defeat him.'

'Defeat? But you said you weren't going to fight.' Topher recognised Bartolomé's voice, and the scornful laugh which followed.

Cortes said, 'Have you not heard of Victory without Battle, Brother Bartolomé? It is an old and noble aim. Most tribes will welcome us when they know we are going to liberate them from Aztec tyranny. And if our plan goes well Montezuma will fall to his knees and worship me.'

'But I'll sharpen my sword and stock up with gunpowder in case he doesn't,' said El Sol. 'I'm not sure those tribes will be welcoming, and it'll take more than a few quetzal feathers to convince Montezuma.'

Once again Topher was mystified. What was El Sol talking about?

'We will be prepared for anything,' replied Cortes. 'But aim to proceed without bloodshed, theirs or ours. Fighting wastes time and resources. We are there to get gold. Gold, remember! Think of that when the going gets hard. Gold!'

'And God,' said Bartolomé, and there was silence for a moment, before talk turned to Tenochtitlan.

That was the city in the middle of a lake, where Montezuma lived. How would they approach it? Cortes asked for Martin Lopez, the boat builder, to stay behind. Then the meeting broke up.

'Hear that, Ka?' Topher stroked Ka who was asleep on the table. 'The master wants new boats, and they could be used for sailing back to Spain!'

Then the door opened and there was El Sol.

'Hear all that, did you? Does the cat want to eat from a golden dish?' He went as if to stroke Ka who hissed at him. 'Haven't forgiven me, I see. Not a good Christian then? I wager you're in league with the devil, witch's cat.'

From then on Ka kept even closer to Topher, and next day, she was with him when they heard the sound of drums and flutes.

'Come on, Ka!' Topher led the way to the front of the house. 'It's the maize god's procession!'

They saw it coming into the square, led by a posse of Aztec priests with matted hair and long black cloaks – in a cloud of flies because priests never washed. Behind them was Nico's sister. It must be her, she looked so much like him, even wearing a long green tunic of green and gold and a headdress of golden corncobs. Poor girl, surrounded by stinking priests! How could she stand it? Four more priests walked behind her, carrying the dough image of the maize god on their shoulders. Oh dear. The statue was dressed like her, but its face was nothing like. Nico's sister didn't have eyes made of emeralds, or teeth made of maize! Would the Indians be satisfied if they sacrificed that?

'Topher! Stop skiving and come here!' It was Cortes' chamberlain in the front doorway. 'Your master wants you to deliver a letter. Put on his livery and report to him in the salon.'

When Topher reported for duty, Cortes was at his writing table. Sweeping his eyes over Topher's striped doublet and hose, he said, 'Good. Your plumed hat too.' Then he turned back to the chamberlain, standing by his desk. 'Listen to this, de Guzman. *Very High and Powerful, Most Excellent Majesties, King Carlos and Queen Juana. As I embark on a dangerous journey to the city of Tenochtitlan, home of the tyrant Montezuma, to make him your vassal, I dedicate everything I do, everything I find, indeed, every breath I take, to God, your gracious majesties and the glory of Spain...'*

De Guzman nodded and swayed – he was very tall – as Cortes read to the end of the letter. Then he handed Cortes a quill. 'Excellent, Governor General, very clear. All you need to do now is sign it.'

Cortes signed with a flourish, reading aloud, '*Your obedient and loyal servant, Hernan Cortes.* That should teach the Governor of Cuba to call me traitor!' He sanded the ink, rolled the parchment and sealed it. 'Topher, take this to Juan de Escalante, whom I have made Sheriff of Veracruz while I am away. Tell him to keep it safe and get it to the King of Spain by the first vessel to call at Veracruz. And – ' Cortes picked up another scroll. 'Take this copy also to de Escalante. If the Governor of Cuba is so unwise as to send an armada to arrest me while I am away, de Escalante need only show its leader this. It's proof positive that I am acting for the crown, and will protect Veracruz from attack.'

As Topher set off for de Escalante's house near the town gates, he wished he were going in the other direction, so he could see the Maize Festival. But what he'd heard had cheered him up. His master was the King of Spain's loyal subject. He was going to get gold for the King. He'd keep some for himself of course, all the conquistadors expected to get rich, but Cortes wasn't setting himself up as King of New Spain.

Even better, when he reached de Escalante's door, a servant said that he was at the temple, watching the Maize Seed Festival. So he turned round and raced back, sorry only that he couldn't take off his thick brocade doublet, for the sun was shining. It was very hot, too hot for Ka, who had stayed behind in Cortes' cool salon. But he might still be in time to see the climax of the Maize Festival and the sacrifice of the dough image.

As he got closer the music got faster and louder, drums, flutes, bells and clashing cymbals and something else which roared like thunder. It sounded as if an important moment was fast approaching. Soon he could see the little thatched building on top of the pyramid and – in gaps between buildings – figures on the steps leading up to it. But as he reached the square, the music stopped. There was silence. Everything, bells, drums, cymbals, everything stopped – and Topher saw the church door opening, and the black habit of a friar hurrying out of it.

Seeing Topher, he beckoned. It was Bartolomé.

'Come,' he said as Topher joined him. 'Let's see if we have succeeded.' And he headed down an alley beside the church into the stadium in front of the pyramid.

The stadium was about twice as big as the town square and it was packed with Indians, mostly Totonacs.

All their eyes were on the pyramid at the far end. Topher looked for de Escalante, thinking he'd be on some sort of raised stand. But there was no stand, nor could he see the front of the crowd. There were far too many people looking at what was happening on the summit. But what exactly was happening up there? He could see human figures moving about but not what they were doing.

Bartolomé nudged him and pointed to a row of weird statues, bordering the stadium. They looked a bit like birds or animals and some wore feathered cloaks.

'Let's get behind those.'

'But I've got to deliver these scrolls.'

'Later. See how things turn out. If the crowd get angry you might need to make a quick exit.'

In his red and gold livery, Topher was quite well hidden behind an owl-like statue, painted similar colours. So was Bartolomé in his black habit, when he stood in its shadow. Topher pulled his hat over his ears to hide his fair hair. The crowd wasn't as silent as he first thought. There were murmurings. People were asking questions:

'What is the image for?'

'Why are the priests carrying it?'

'Why didn't they carry the maiden as usual?'

'Why the change? Where is the real maiden?'

'Ah, there she is!'

Topher couldn't see if they were right. They seemed to think Patti was up there on the summit, but they were worried. Things were different. What would the gods think? The atmosphere was tense. He strained his eyes to see the top of the pyramid – and saw a spurt of blood.

Real blood? The crowd gasped and then sighed. There were more murmurings – which seemed to be of approval. Yes. The sigh was *relief*! The god's will was done. All would be well now. When blood starting to trickle down the steps of the pyramid, he could feel their satisfaction. But he didn't know what to think. Was that paint or was it Patti's blood? There was a lot of it.

Drums began to beat as a red river poured down the steps. And now the crowd surged forward. Some of them began to climb the steps. Two black-clad priests pushed them back. More pushed past and one of them reached whatever it was that was dripping onto the lower steps.

'This is the test.' Bartolomé was looking through a telescope. 'He's dipping his hands in it. Smearing it on his face. Tasting it.'

'Does he think it's real?'

He didn't hear the answer because someone was poking, no pulling, him.

'Nico!' His face was almost as white as Topher's.

'Come.' He yanked Topher's arm – and the scrolls fell onto the ground.

'No, Nico.' Topher picked them up. 'I must deliver these.'

'Later. I need your help.' Nico's eyes were pleading. 'Listen. Things are going wrong.'

'He's right,' said Bartolomé. 'They know it's not blood.'

The crowd sounded angry.

'Please,' said Nico. He started to push his way forward through the crowd, who were still focused on the pyramid.

68

And Topher followed though he wasn't sure where he was going or why.

It soon became clear. Nico was heading for the back of the pyramid. They reached it and he pointed to the summit. 'Up.'

'What *for*, Nico?' Topher was puffed out. He'd already run from one end of the town to the other.

'For Patti of course. They *know*. Can't you hear? The crowd knows she isn't dead.'

From the other side of the pyramid came a rhythmic chant.

'Sacr-i-fice!'

'Sacr-i-fice!'

And there were other people up there.

Nico's face was creased with anguish. 'We've got to get to her before they do.'

He started climbing again and Topher followed, scrambling up the huge stone steps, passing doorways and passageways that he hadn't noticed before.

Nico hissed, 'Keep down! We mustn't be seen from the other side.'

Topher thought – we've probably *been* seen from the inside – as the chant speeded up.

'Sacr-i-fice! Sacr-i-fice!'

'Kill the girl! Kill the girl!'

The crowd were mad for blood.

'Where is she, Nico?'

'Up here somewhere.'

Then they saw something dark on the step above and froze.

A shadow? A bundle of black cloth? A...?

Topher glanced at Nico whose face paled.

Then the bundle sat up.

'Francisco!'

'Don't worry, Nico. I've got her.' The fat friar lifted his habit – and there was Patti.

But there was no time for rejoicing.

The monk said, 'Topher, give me your clothes.'

'But...?'

'For Patti. Quick. You put this on.' Francisco pulled off the top half of his black habit and dropped it over Topher's head. Darkness, as he struggled to undress enveloped in Francisco's enormous habit. Other hands were trying to help him.

'No. I'll do it myself!' And he did.

When he emerged Patti was in his doublet and hose and Nico was stuffing her hair under Topher's hat. She seemed stunned. Drugged, she must be. Nico grasped her shoulders and looked into her eyes. 'Go with Topher,' he said firmly. 'He will take you to safety.' He put her hand in Topher's. 'Take her to Bartolomé. But you'll have to guide her, lead the way.'

She was like a sleepwalker. As Topher led her down the steps he saw Indians swarming round the side of the pyramid. And there was a crowd at the base watching their descent. Waiting for him? Waiting for her? Hoping he could get her to Bartolomé who might know what to do, he kept moving and he had an idea. When they were nearly at the bottom he pulled back his shoulders and straightened to his full height. Then he put his arm round

Patti, making sure that the wide sleeve of his habit covered her face, *his* face. Did she look like a boy? Did he look like a monk? At least he was taller than her. *Him.* He must remember.

'Make way, please,' he said in Nahuatl, making his voice as deep and manly as he could. 'The boy is ill. I am taking him to the infirmary,'

The Indians shuffled backwards.

'Ill. Ill.' The word went round and they kept their distance. Nothing frightened them more than the white man's illnesses. Measles. Pox. They had killed even more than the white man's firesticks. Now, steering Patti as best he could, Topher moved a bit faster, heading for the row of statues bordering the crowded stadium, and keeping a lookout for Bartolomé. As the monk wasn't near the eagle statue, he headed for the church, but as he tried to manoeuvre Patti down the narrow alley towards the back door of the church, she began to struggle.

'Where you take me?' She pulled away from him.

'A safe place.' He hung on to her, and managed to reach the door's bell rope.

But the bar remained in place.

He pulled the bell again. The bar went up, the door opened and there was Bartolomé. He drew them both inside.

'Did anyone see you come here?'

'Don't know. I told people she – he – was ill.'

'Good thinking.' Bartolomé turned to Patti and spoke to her gently in Nahuatl. But she wasn't pleased to be rescued. With dark eyes darting round the room looking for escape, she looked like a trapped deer.

Bartolomé said, 'Topher, the situation is dangerous. I think you should go and tell Cortes what is happening.'

Cortes! Hearing his master's name, Topher remembered the letters for de Escalante and his blood ran cold.

Chapter 11

Where were they? Topher tried not to panic, but if he had lost the letters Cortes would be furious. It would mean a beating or worse. He'd put them down when he'd swapped clothes with Patti. Not swapped exactly. Patti was still in his clothes, but he was still wearing Francisco's habit.

'Bartolomé, I've got to go. I've left something at the pyramid.'

Bartolomé saw the urgency. 'Go, but be careful.'

'Like this? Or in my own clothes?'

What would be safest? Were the Indians more likely to attack a monk or a Spanish boy wearing Cortes' livery? He remembered his lie about Patti being ill. It had worked. He spoke to her in Nahuatl. 'Please, may I have my clothes?'

'Where are my clothes?' she replied.

He had no idea. Nor had Bartolomé. Whatever plan they'd had to save Patti had gone wrong.

There was a knock on the door. They froze.

'Who's there?' Bartolomé peered through the latch-hole, his hand grasping the cord.

'Me. Nico. Open up.'

Bartolomé pulled the cord and the door opened.

Nico darted inside with a bundle and spoke to Patti rapidly in Nahuatl. Then he took her behind a screen.

Moments later Topher's doublet came flying over. Hose and hat followed and it didn't take Topher long to put them on, but he needed one more thing.

'Bartolomé, may I go to your house?'

'What for?'

'Chili powder. For a red rash – so I'll be left alone.'

It didn't take long to find the spice in Francisco's tiny cooking area, or blotch his face with damp fingers, taking care to keep the fiery stuff out of his eyes or mouth. Then he set off for the stadium, running at first, but slowing to a staggering walk when he got there, trying to look like someone who was ill.

The stadium was still full of Indians. They obviously thought Patti was still on the pyramid and might yet be sacrificed. Someone threw him a hostile glance, but recoiled when they saw his spots. Good. But there was no point in drawing more attention to himself. He retreated to the edge of the crowd where the statues gave better cover. It didn't take him long to reach the back of the pyramid. There were still people up there too, Indians he thought, though he couldn't see well. But were the scrolls up there? He couldn't see. They were small and parchment was the same colour as the steps. There were more Indians at the foot of the pyramid. Would they try to stop him climbing up? He felt their stares as he put his foot on the first step, heard someone say, 'He shouldn't be doing that.' Heard another say, 'Stop him.' But no one did. Then when he was about halfway up someone shouted – in Spanish.

'Topher!' It came from below. 'Stop!'

Looking down, he saw three men on horseback, and one had yellow hair.

'Here, boy! Now!' El Sol ordered him to descend.

The new sheriff and another conquistador were beside him.

'Faster!' El Sol roared.

Topher nearly slid down, and landed at the feet of El Sol's horse.

El Sol seemed amused – till he saw Topher's face. 'Are you ill?'

'Yes. No. Not really.' He hoped no Indians could understand.

'You're wearing Cortes' livery. Were you on his business?'

'Yes, Capitan de Alvarado.' He remembered El Sol's proper name.

'Doing what?'

What could he say? He felt his face going redder.

El Sol smirked. 'Was it something to do with this?' He pointed to a scroll in the sheriff's hand.

All three commanders seemed to be enjoying some sort of joke.

'Careless, Topher.' El Sol went on. 'It was lucky that I spotted it.' He tapped the telescope that hung from his belt. 'Cortes would not be pleased if he knew how careless you'd been, would he?'

'No, Capitan de Alvarado.'

'Then you must hope we don't tell him.'

Topher felt sick. El Sol could and would tell Cortes whenever he wanted.

De Escalante sounded more sympathetic. 'All's well that ends well, eh? Tell Cortes that I will do my very best to get his letter to the King of Spain.'

'Yes, Sheriff de Escalante. Thank you.'

'And thank me,' said El Sol, 'for finding and delivering the letter to the right person. Don't you think you owe me a little gratitude, Topher? A little more respect?'

'Yes. Thank you, Capitan de Alvarado.'

'Good. Well, run along and tell the Governor General you have carried out his orders. And tell him I have the town under control, even though the Dominican do-gooders have stopped the natives having their fun.'

As Topher made his escape, he noticed more conquistadors among the crowd, with swords drawn and arquebuses at the ready. So that's why none of the Indians had stopped him climbing the pyramid. But something still wasn't right. El Sol had said he'd delivered '*the letter*' to de Escalante. Why not 'letters'? There had been two scrolls. Could '*the letter*' mean he'd handed over two copies of '*the letter*' that Cortes had written? If so why had de Escalante said he'd get the letter to the king? Why hadn't he mentioned the copy for the Governor of Cuba? Was there one scroll or two in his hand? One could have been wrapped round the other – but if there were two, wouldn't he have mentioned the other one? Wouldn't he have said he'd keep it safe in case the Governor of Cuba arrived with an army? The more Topher thought about it, the more convinced he became that El Sol had kept the other. But why? Did El Sol want an attack on Veracruz while Cortes was away? Why would he want that?

Topher reached the road that ran along the back of the stadium. Which way now? He ought to turn right and go straight to Cortes, but if he went back to the church he could ask Bartolomé for advice. But he was late already – and there was no need to ask Bartolomé. He knew what he would say. *Own up, Topher. Be honest!* And that was the right thing to do, even if it meant a beating. At a stroke – or several – it would forestall any mischief of El Sol's. And make him angry perhaps? But confessing was the right thing to do. Now Topher speeded up, had to force himself not to break into a run. An Indian sweeping the street looked at him suspiciously. If only he had a bell to shake like a leper. Out of my way. Out of my way. Now he was keen to get back and do the right thing. If he told Cortes that one of his letters had gone astray, Cortes could take steps to find it.

But Cortes wasn't at home. It was Doña Marina who greeted him as he hesitated in the doorway of the salon, waiting for his eyes to adjust from dazzling sunlight to the darkness of the room. At first he did not see her, then he heard her voice and there she was on the far side of the room by a window.

'Where have you been?' As she stepped out of the shadows, she looked and sounded like a Spanish lady. Her yellow dress made of Indian cotton was full skirted in the Spanish style, and her heavy black hair was held high on her head with combs.

'I have been delivering letters to the sheriff.'

'And why have you been so long?'

'Because he was not at his house and I had to go and

77

look for him.'

'But you did deliver the letters?'

'Yes . . . ' *But maybe only one* – the words didn't come out. Something about the look she gave him staunched the flow.

'Good, because if you had not, I would have had you skinned alive. Now hurry out of your livery and into your working clothes. There is much to do before we leave for Tenochtitlan.'

Skinned alive! As he scrambled upstairs to change Topher couldn't get her words out of his head. Isn't that what Aztecs did? Skinned people – while they were still alive – with their little stone knives? And Doña Marina was an Aztec born and bred, though she now looked like a Spanish lady. As soon as he could, he raced to Ka in the armoury, tidy now thanks to his efforts and full of gleaming weapons. The sun was streaming through the window and Ka was basking in its warmth. He buried his face in her fur.

'What should I do, Ka? Tell Cortes the whole truth or hope for the best?'

He felt her purrs.

Tell the trrr . . . uth, Topher. Tell the trrr . . . uth. Tell the trrr . . . uth.

'You're right, Ka. It's better that I tell Cortes myself.'

But it was easier said than done.

Chapter 12

That night Cortes was in a bad mood, because many of his commanders wanted to postpone the expedition to Tenochtitlan. Topher heard them arguing in the salon as he filled and re-filled their cups with red wine.

De Escalante said, 'It is not a good time to leave. The Indians are angry because we have interfered with their festival, and our men are angry because there's a shortage of bread, salt and bacon.'

Most of the conquistadors were farmers or merchants, rich gentlemen, who had come to make themselves richer. They were not used to going without food.

Cortes patted his stomach. 'Am I starving? Are the natives starving? Tell your men to eat what they eat. Get your women to make you tortillas.'

'Tortillas need flour, and stocks are low,' said de Escalante. 'The population of Veracruz has tripled since the last harvest. Flour may well run out before the new crop of maize is harvested. Our men have other worries too – about the heat of the jungle and the cold of the mountains. Some say it is so cold at the top that parts of your body freeze and drop off.'

'They are afraid of dying,' said another commander, ignoring Cortes' drumming fingers. 'They think the expedition too risky.'

'Of course it's risky!' Cortes exploded. 'Nothing

venture nothing win! I thought they came for adventure and gold! Are they men or mice? We leave in three days' time. Make sure everything is ready!'

But they didn't leave in three days' time. They didn't leave for three months, because Doña Marina changed Cortes' mind, and Topher and Ka were there when she did it. Next morning, she asked Topher to carry two large scrolls to the salon, where Cortes was sitting at his desk.

'My lord.' He looked up at her words. 'May I show you something important?'

Topher helped unfurl the scrolls and hold them flat. Doña Marina pointed to two circular diagrams, each covered with Aztec picture writing.

'Aztec calendars,' she said. 'See, we have two different ones. This one, showing the agricultural year has 365 days, like the Christian year. The other, showing the sacred year has 260 days.'

Cortes sighed. 'And why are they important, Marina?'

She picked up one diagram and laid it over the other. 'Because they show us the best day to arrive in Tenochtitlan. See.' She turned up the edge of the top one and pointed to one segment. 'By an amazing good fortune, this year 1519 in Christian calendar, is auspicious year in Aztec calendar. On only one day, every fifty-two years, do the two Aztec calendars, the agricultural and the sacred, come together – and that will happen this year, Year of the Reed, on what the Aztecs called the Day of the Wind, Quetzalcoatl's day. And, my lord, with my help you will arrive as the long-awaited god, Quetzalcoatl, on that very day! It is the eighth day of November in the Christian calendar!'

'But that is months away!'

'Six months, my lord – it is now May – so we have time to prepare properly!'

As Topher listened he began to understand the plan. Cortes was going to pretend to be Quetzalcoatl, a white-skinned Aztec god, who had left earth five hundred years ago, promising to appear from the east one day and rule over them. Aztec priests expected Quetzalcoatl to arrive on his special day – in six months' time, so telling Cortes about the letter wasn't urgent.

It seemed like a good plan, peaceful anyway. And it looked as if it might work, for later that day envoys from Montezuma arrived and they said Montezuma was looking forward to Cortes' visit. They had come, they said, as guides, to show Cortes the best route, and to bring him gifts. One emptied a sack full of little gold animals at his feet. Another gave him a basket full of gold bells and bangles. Another put a jade necklace round his neck and a cloak of quetzal feather round his shoulders.

'These gifts may be a sign that Montezuma thinks you are Quetzalcoatl,' Doña Marina said. 'Or they may not. We must not believe everything they say. We will choose our own route. I think you need the Tlaxcalans, who are the Aztecs' fiercest enemies, on your side. It is a longer route through their territory but it will be worthwhile. Let us send Jeronimo with gifts to negotiate a safe passage with the chief of their tribe.'

As ever she was practical. 'It is wise to wait for the harvest,' she said. 'If it is good, the natives will calm down and may even become Christians. And there will be bread for the journey.'

When Jeronimo returned he had a promise of five hundred Tlaxcalan warriors – and it looked as if there would be a good harvest. Corncobs were growing fat in the Indians' tidy gardens. Cortes sent Topher to check on them regularly. Sometimes he saw Nico. Sometimes he even joined in with a ballgame – though not in the special court sacred to the gods – and he met yet another brother of Nico's, a shy boy called Naxos.

'How is your sister?' Topher asked them one day, during a break in the game.

'She is in place of safety,' Nico replied.

'Is that still necessary now the maize has grown so well?' The hot rainy weather had been good for that at least.

'My parents are still fearful. Some people are still angry that she not die.'

Topher noticed Nico crossing himself.

'Have you become a Christian, Nico?'

'Yes. Father Sahagun baptised me.'

But Nico didn't let that stop him playing in the sacred ballgame, when the harvest had been collected in.

He and three of his brothers played for the Sun team, and they beat the Moons 14–5 with Naxos, who was very quick, getting nine of the goals. But when the rest of the team tried to lift him high and carry him round the court – they were so happy to win – he ran off.

'He is very – how you say? – shy,' said Nico.

'But fast,' said Topher. 'Is he coming with us on the expedition?'

'We do not know yet.'

'Doesn't he want to come? I thought all of you did.'

Most Totonac boys were desperate to go, so they could kill Aztecs. A boy could only call himself a man when he had killed in battle. Before that he had to wear his hair long like a girl, except that girls wore coloured ribbons round their hair. But when a boy had killed in battle his hair was cut short, except for a few strands on top, the famous topknot. All the boys seemed to think they would get lots of opportunities in Tenochtitlan.

Topher didn't tell them they might not. Envoys arrived nearly every day with gifts from Montezuma, and Cortes talked a lot about Victory without Battle. One envoy brought him a dragon's head made of gold, and placed it on his head like a crown. Cortes said it was a sign that Montezuma would welcome him, and hand over power and more gold when he arrived in Tenochtitlan. The date for departure was set, August 16th. That gave the expedition two months to reach Lake Texcoco, and a month to build ships to carry them to the floating city of Tenochtitlan in the middle of the lake.

On the day before they set off for Tenochtitlan Topher put Ka in the travelling basket he'd had made for her, and she seemed content.

'I don't want you to think of it as a cage, Ka.'

Don't worry. Don't worry. She purred as he reached in to stroke her.

83

'You can walk sometimes. But not all the way, or you'd wear out your paws.'

She rubbed her cheek against his hand.

'I just wish Bartolomé and Francisco were coming with us.'

They couldn't because Cortes had decided they should take his letter to the King of Spain, by the first ship that called at Veracruz.

Don't worry. Don't worry.

For Topher had started to worry. How would Cortes convert the Aztecs to Christianity without Bartolomé and Francisco, while pretending to be an Aztec god? The plan, which had seemed good at first, seemed not so good now. Perhaps the plan had changed? Cortes often changed his mind. If he wanted Victory without Battle why were the conquistadors taking so many weapons? Why were they packing so much gunpowder? Why were they going to drag six heavy cannon over the mountains? And why were they taking so many Indian warriors, all eager for war? Nico and all his brothers were coming – that was good – but would they all come back?

Chapter 13

But next morning as he listened to his master's voice ringing out over the square, his doubts vanished. Cortes looked magnificent in his shining armour, as he sat on the back of Diablo. And Doña Marina looked wonderful with her long black hair and scarlet cape flowing over her mount's back.

'Gentlemen! The moment we have long awaited has arrived! Now let us follow the banner, the sign of the Holy Cross and by this shall we conquer!' *Conquer. Conquer.* His voice bounced off the surrounding buildings, and the blue and white banner with its red cross flew high as the standard bearer held it aloft.

'Some of you may be fearful,' Cortes continued, 'but do not be fearful. Some of you may fear death.' *Death. Death.* The word echoed round the square. 'But do not fear death, for we go as gods and we go *for* God. And if we die – and some of us may, bravely, as is our way – we die as gods, to rise again, in Heaven where God will welcome us for we are about His work!'

A great cheer greeted these rousing words.

'What would we do without our leader?'

Topher, stooping to check Ka in the basket at his feet, wasn't surprised to see El Sol sneering down at him from his chestnut mare.

'Let us pray that nothing untoward happens to him, for

then you would have to polish my armour and make it sparkle. Would you like that, Topher?'

But he went with a kick of his heels before Topher could answer.

'What was El Sol saying?' Bartolomé joined Topher a few minutes later, and when Topher told him, the monk looked concerned. 'Be wary, Topher. There is good in all men, but not as much as I would like in El Sol.'

'Bartolomé, I wish you were coming.'

The monk picked up Ka's basket. 'Have faith. Father Sahagun will do his best to remind our leader of the holy purpose of the expedition. Now come. General Cortes is leading off. We must find the baggage cart, unless you want to walk all the way.'

'Why is he going that way?' The town gates were in the opposite direction.

'Because he's going to the pyramid first, to hand the town keys to de Escalante, publicly, so that everyone knows he is in charge. You know de Escalante is going to live in the Aztec priests' quarters inside the pyramid to show the Indians he is boss? Cortes is taking no chances. He doesn't want trouble here while he's away.'

The company, in seven brigades each of a hundred and fifty men, was moving forward slowly. Most were on foot. Only the brigade leaders had horses – and Cortes' closest servants. Caceres the major-domo and de Guzman the chamberlain were carrying a rolled-up carpet between them, for Cortes to rest on after each meal. The two priests had a mount between them. Father Sahagun was on it now. Where was the baggage cart? Indians were carrying most

86

of the food and ammunition on their backs.

'Over there, Topher!' Bartolomé pointed to a cart with four Indians harnessed to it like horses. He handed him Ka's basket. 'And now I must leave you.' He grasped Topher's other hand, held it for a moment and looked deep into his eyes. 'God go with you – and remember what I said.'

Then he was gone, and it was as if the sun had gone behind a cloud.

As Topher wedged Ka's basket in the back of the cart, between bundles of bedding, he thought about Bartolomé's warning. How could he be wary? How could he protect himself and Ka from El Sol?

'What can we do, Ka?'

'Mi-aow!' Her eyes blazed, and he remembered the lost letter, which he'd never managed to speak about.

'Is that all you can say?'

'Mi-aOW!' *You know what I mean.* She started to scratch the sides.

'Stop that. You'll make a hole in the reeds.'

'Mi-aOW! MI-AOW-OW!'

'I can't, Ka. I can't. Cortes says you must stay there. I *am* staying with you.'

But that didn't please her. Something else was making her angry. As he climbed onto the cart, she turned her back on him and stayed like that till they reached the stadium.

De Escalante was on the pyramid steps, which had been scraped and scrubbed, but there was still a stain where the blood had been. De Escalante was flanked by the hundred conquistadors who were staying with him to keep order in Veracruz. To the side of them was a group of Aztec priests roped together. At the base of the pyramid three cannon were aimed at the packed stadium. As Cortes handed over the keys he made a speech.

'From this moment on, he who offends the sheriff offends me. He who offends the sheriff will be punished as if by me, even to the losing of life itself. I leave you now to go and lift the Aztec yoke from your shoulders!'

Doña Marina translated his words into Nahuatl. Then the new sheriff bade them farewell, and walked up the steps into the pyramid.

Now Topher smelt the priests, as they were led out from the pyramid to stand behind the baggage cart, for they were going to Tenochtitlan as hostages. They would be brought back alive only if there was no trouble from the Indians while Cortes was away. As Bartolomé said, Cortes was taking no chances.

So, thought Topher, his master must have checked that de Escalante had the letter for the Governor of Cuba. Must have. It must be safe in a desk somewhere in the pyramid. Must be. If an armada from Cuba arrived he would produce the letter and forestall an attack. Of course he would. Topher had convinced himself, but not Ka.

'Ow!' Blood spurted from his hand. She had scratched him! 'What did you do that for?'

She was hissing, *Sss-stupid, sss-stupid, sss-stupid*, her eyes blazing scorn.

Then the cart moved forward. They were off at last. He heard Doña Marina say, 'See yonder mountain? In ten days' time we will be on the other side!'

But in ten days' time they were stuck in the jungle.

Chapter 14

'Cat out.'

At first Topher thought it was Nico speaking – it was hard to see in the jungle – even in this clearing where the company had camped. But it was Nico's brother, Naxos, the one who was so good at the ballgame. The white cloth round his middle stood out against the leaves. So did his teeth and the whites of his eyes, but his skin and hair were lost in the darkness. He often came to see Ka and always said the same thing. *Cat out. Cat out.* And Topher always made the same reply. *My master says no, something might catch her.* And now he agreed with his master. What if one of those strange monkeys or huge cats grabbed her?

They had been in the jungle for days now, and though Topher wore a cloth round his middle too, he still felt sick with the heat and, yes, scared. The jungle was dark as night and full of strange noises.

'Cat out. Let cat out.' Naxos was learning their language fast. He crouched by Ka's basket, putting his fingers through the bars. And Ka let him stroke her, though she hadn't let Topher touch her for days. When he tried, she shot to the back of the basket, but now she was rubbing her cheeks against Naxos's fingers and rippling with pleasure. *I like you. Naxos. Please let me out and I will live with you.*

'But you might get caught by something.'

Naxos looked up. 'Why quiet?'

'Don't know.'

It had suddenly gone quiet. But only moments ago the sounds of chopping and crashing had drowned out the screeching of parrots and macaws, for the conquistadors were clearing a new track through the jungle.

'We go Jalapa town?' said Naxos.

'Yes, but by new road.' Cortes suspected an ambush on the road that was already there. That's why the journey was taking longer than planned. He kept changing the plan.

'Why you not let cat out?' Naxos was fondling Ka's ears.

'Because Cortes says I cannot.'

Ka purred.

'I think she stay near if you let out. I see her follow in Veracruz like chihuahua.'

Ka stopped purring. *How dare you compare me to a dog?* And Topher smiled because he read her thoughts. 'She says she's not a dog.'

'Good,' said Naxos. 'I no like your dogs.'

'Nor do I.'

The pack of wolfhounds the conquistadors had brought with them was scary, even on leashes. Let loose in battle they terrified the Indians even more than horses.

Naxos produced a ball from somewhere. 'Topher, we play?'

'Sorry, Naxos, I have to tidy my master's shelter. You help me?'

'No!' Naxos shook his head.

90

'But you helped yesterday.' He had shaken the bedrolls, rolled them tightly to keep out termites and put them tidily in the shelter.

'No!' He disappeared, till leaves the size of platters started to flutter down from a tree above. Then Topher saw him up a tree pointing to a looped branch.

'Here!' He dropped the ball down. 'Throw!'

Topher aimed and scored – and Naxos shouted something in Nahuatl that sounded like hurrah! But when Topher missed he laughed so much he nearly fell from the tree. He was more fun than his brothers.

'Where's Nico by the way?' The brothers usually stuck together.

'Fight Aztecs.'

'Practising, you mean? Why you not with them?'

But Naxos had his head on one side. 'You hear war cries?'

'Maybe.' War cries or parrot cries – he couldn't tell the difference.

Naxos laughed. 'White man no hear good.'

'Or smell good.' Topher laughed. 'Doña Marina says we stink. She makes Captain Cortes wash every day with – what you call it – ahuacatl?' It was a fruit!

'Doña Marina Aztec. I Totomac.' Naxos was peering into the baggage cart. 'But Doña Marina right.' He held his nose. 'You dirty, we clean.'

He'd got a whiff of Cortes' clothes, which Topher was supposed to look after. But they'd started to go mouldy as soon as he'd packed them away, when Cortes started wearing clothes like the Indians'. Topher picked up his best brocade doublet, black with mildew. 'How do I get that clean, Naxos?'

But the boy had gone, silently, like a shadow. Topher thought he saw him running between the trees.

Then Nico appeared. 'Topher, you must not ask Naxos to do . . . *housework*.' The last word was a grimace.

'Housework?' Topher tried to joke. 'I see no houses.' Shelters yes, made of branches and leaves.

'Housework – in our tribe' – Nico looked serious – 'that woman's work.'

Topher sighed. 'In my tribe too, Nico. Haven't you heard the conquistadors mocking me? But there are not many women here, so I look after my master's things, like I did on the ship when I was his cabin boy.'

'But do not ask Naxos to help.'

'But he's so good . . . '

'NO, Topher! It shameful!' He hid his face behind his hands. And Topher remembered Doña Marina saying, 'Have you got a little Indian girlfriend, Topher?' when she found the shelter neat and tidy, her things one side, Cortes' on the other, in the Indian way.

Topher touched his arm. 'Don't worry. I will not ask him again.'

Nico smiled. 'If you want shelter? Building, that is man's work.'

'Thank you, Nico, but I like the hammock you made me.'

It was in the trees, above Cortes' shelter in case he called in the night. Nico and Naxos had woven it for him from vines and lined it with leaves.

'I go now.' Nico vanished into the trees, and El Sol, looking hot in doublet and hose, stepped out from behind the shelter. *How long had he been there?*

'What's upset your Indian amigo, Topher?'

'He doesn't like his brother helping me with my chores.'

'Which brother?'

'Naxos.'

El Sol smirked and stroked his gold-streaked beard. 'Good at them, isn't he? Have you ever thought why? Oh dear. You're not very clever, are you, Topher? But are you clever enough to find our leader's compass? He needs it to check the direction of the new track, or impress the natives with a bit of white man's magic.'

Topher got it from the chest at the back of the baggage cart, and El Sol studied the dial for a bit. 'Next time you see your Indian amigo look a little closer. But don't tell the others what you see – unless you want to cause trouble.' Then he closed the compass lid and strode off grinning. What did he mean?

Chapter 15

There was trouble enough already. It took them days to reach Jalapa where they were supposed to rest and stock up with supplies, before climbing over the mountain which overlooked the town. Fever slowed them down. Already several Indians and two conquistadors had died of it, and two more Indians had been killed as they cleared the new track. They'd been shot in their spines by arrows. That's why work had stopped for a bit, while everyone searched for the killers. But they got away. No one even saw them. Cortes suspected Montezuma. He thought he was trying to stop him reaching Tenochtitlan. And when they did reach Jalapa, the town chief, standing on the steps of the pyramid, seemed to confirm his fears.

Cortes asked, 'Are you a vassal of Montezuma?'

The chief replied, 'Is not everyone a vassal of Montezuma? Is he not ruler of the world?'

'No,' said Cortes. 'I am a greater lord and will make Montezuma bow before me!'

The turquoise paint on the chief's face was so thick it was impossible to read his expression, but he said, 'I have orders from Montezuma to treat you as honoured guests. Honour me by staying in my palace.' And his followers garlanded Cortes and Doña Marina with flowers.

The palace was beautiful with many rooms, built round courtyards with fountains, which played all day and night. The water was piped in from the mountains.

'If only we stay here,' said Naxos next morning. He had brought a lead for Ka, made of plaited reeds – and Cortes had said she could leave her basket if she wore it.

'The conquistadors don't want to stay,' said Topher. 'They think they are going to be poisoned. Last night the chief held a great feast but many of them wouldn't eat. But I too wish we could stay.'

But two days later, they set off again, up a mountain path, which would lead them to the land of the Tlaxcalans on the other side.

Now the road rose steeply and the track was only wide enough for men to walk in single file. It was too narrow for the carts, which kept breaking down. More and more stuff was piled on the Indians' backs and they had to drag the cannon up the mountainside, harnessed to it like animals. More of them died, from fever or exhaustion or cold, for the higher they got, the colder it got. Summer turned to winter, suddenly it seemed.

The conquistadors changed back into their Spanish clothes, but most of the Indians didn't have thick clothes. A few had brought padded cotton armour to wear in battle, but most only had loin clothes and little capes made from cactus fibre.

And it snowed. Many had never seen snow before, not close up. Now swirling snow froze their half naked bodies. More died, Indians and conquistadors. Others saw their fingers and toes turn black then drop off. And the cold got worse. The snow cut their skin with icy bullets, flayed it with icy blades. And the snowstorms went on and on and on, so they lost track of night and day, and Cortes forbade them to stop anyway, for fear of freezing solid if they lay down or even stood still.

Then, gradually – no one knew how long it took – it began to get warmer, the wind dropped, and they thought they might have reached the other side. When the snow under their feet became thinner, Cortes announced that the worst was over and allowed them to halt. But now, as they made camp, the complaints began, bitter complaints – about Cortes – for people blamed him for the death of their comrades. Worse, there was no food left or water, so they feared for their own lives.

Quickly and loudly El Sol stepped in to stem the criticism. Topher heard him. So did Cortes and Doña Marina, as El Sol intended them to. They had all made camp. Cortes' brigade were sheltering as best they could, under an overhanging rock. El Sol and his brigade were close by and his Indians were cursing Cortes.

'Do not blame the Captain General!' El Sol urged them. 'Do not blame your leader. Captain Cortes cares for you as much as he cares for the white men he brought with him – and see none of them have died.'

That was not true. Several had died, even before the snow, but they'd been buried secretly at night, on Cortes' orders, to give the impression that white men, like gods, didn't die.

'Think about why you are suffering,' El Sol went on. 'Have you perhaps done something to make your gods angry? Think about what you have done, or not done, and how you could make amends.'

Who did he want them to blame? Topher knew. And so did Nico and his brothers who appeared next morning. They all rejoiced because they hadn't seen each other for several days. Then Nico said he and his brothers were worried because El Sol was stirring up trouble.

Topher nodded. 'I know. It is fortunate that Patti isn't with us.'

And Nico said nothing, but something clicked in Topher's head, as he saw Naxos staring at the ground. Suddenly he remembered El Sol saying, '*Have a closer look*,' and realised. One look at Nico's face told him he was right, and he wanted to kick himself for not realising earlier. It explained such a lot. Nico's anger at Naxos helping him wash clothes and store the bedroll. Naxos running away from the other players wanting to hoist him – *her* – on their shoulders. For Naxos was Patti and if the other Indians found out they would blame her and her brothers for deceiving them – and they would make another attempt to sacrifice her.

Chapter 16

The weather continued to improve. Soon the path levelled then fell and the terrain turned greener. For a while mist enveloped them, and they had to walk even more carefully, but when the mist cleared they could see a flat plain spreading out beneath them and a gleaming lake. Water! They had drunk all they'd brought with them from Jalapa and eaten all the food, but there were fresh supplies ahead. Now they kept a lookout for a village surrounded by neat fields full of crops. The closer they got to the base of the mountain, the more excited they got, though they couldn't yet see any buildings, or any sign of the waiting Tlaxcalan army, but the weather was getting warmer. It was summer again! Cortes sent El Sol on ahead, to find the Tlaxcalans and tell them the conquistadors were on their way. Topher let Ka walk on her lead. They speeded up despite their thirst, but when they were nearly at the bottom they saw El Sol coming up to meet them. He was waving his arms. Bad news was all over his face and soon they learned what it was.

'The lake is a salt lake,' El Sol reported to Cortes, 'and it is surrounded by salt marshes. The land all round is barren. There are no crops and no fresh water and no waiting Tlaxcalans. Someone has made a mistake.' He glanced at Doña Marina who stood beside Cortes. 'And, as you can see, there is another mountain, straight ahead, on the other side of the lake. Perhaps the Tlaxcalans are on the other side of that, or perhaps they are not.'

It was clear they had further to go than they thought, without food or water.

The days that followed were dreadful. The Indians refused to go west, because the mountain ahead of them was smoking. They said the fire god, Matlacueye, would devour them if they did. So Cortes led them north, though that meant walking round three sides of the lake instead of one. Before they set off he made a speech saying they were sure to find food and water soon. But they didn't. They didn't find food or fresh water all that day or the next. At night they slept on the shores of the lake, and would have sunk into the marsh if the Indians hadn't woven them sleeping mats from reeds.

On the third night Topher couldn't sleep because he thought Ka was going to die. He lay in the darkness and all he could see was her little pink tongue, as she lay on his stomach panting.

'Forgive me, Ka.'

How long could she go without water? Her small body was drying out faster than his. If he'd had spit in his own mouth he would have given it to her, but his mouth was dry, his lips crusty with salt. So he lay staring at the stars, praying she would last till morning. Then it was morning and someone was shaking his arm. He must have slept.

'Wake up. Wake up.'

Naxos, Patti, he, she, no best to think *he*, had something in his hand.

'Ka? Where? Not in basket.' His voice was urgent.

'H-here.' He lifted the cover, and she was lying exactly where he'd put her last night.

But – yes – she was still breathing, but a sticky film covered her eyes.

'Quick! Open mouth.' Naxos-Patti was on her, *his*, knees, holding some sort of plant and a little stone knife. 'Water,' he said. 'You see.' He sliced off the tip of a green shoot and a drop of clear liquid formed on the end, which he held over Ka's mouth till a drop fell onto her tongue.

'Water?' Topher could hardly believe it.

'Yes.'

Another drop fell into Ka's mouth. And another. Drop after drop, almost a trickle, fell from the stem – and Ka's tongue flicked. Yes, she'd got the taste of it and she liked it. And now it was trickling, almost too fast for her to swallow. A drop went down her nose and she sneezed – and looked like Ka again!

Now Naxos cupped his hand. 'Like this. You.'

Topher cupped his hand and Naxos let the water drop into it. Then he lifted Ka so she could drink. Topher saw her tongue come out, felt it rough against his palm as she lapped, messily, as she always did, splashing his fingers!

'Don't waste it, Ka.'

'No worry. Have more.' Naxos got a bunch of the flowery vine from under his cape. He cut off a green shoot and held it out to Topher. 'See. You now! Like this.' He put his head back and held the shoot over his mouth, but Topher didn't need to be shown. He'd got the idea. The liquid was dropping into his mouth. Water!

Delicious fresh water was trickling down his throat!

Word spread quickly. Soon all the conquistadors knew that the Indians had found water. Nico told Cortes that Naxos had found the vine growing among trees about a league inland. He and his brothers had gone looking for it early that morning, and God had been kind. The plant was rare but they had found it. And there was more. He said each cut branch would last for several days. The cut end dried up to preserve the liquid, but if you cut a slice from the stalk once a day, an arm-length piece would yield a quart of water a day.

Cortes sent Nico and Naxos and their brothers to get more supplies. El Sol appeared as they set off.

Cortes said, 'They are true Christians to share this knowledge with us. They could easily have kept it secret and let us die.'

El Sol murmured in his ear. Topher heard the words 'another secret' and guessed what he was saying, even before Cortes said, 'Is this true, Topher, that Naxos is the girl they didn't sacrifice?'

Topher nodded and his heart sank. The game was up.

But Cortes went on. 'No one, I mean *no one*, must be told about this.' He turned to El Sol. 'I trust you have told no one?'

El Sol shook his head and Topher hoped he wasn't lying.

'She, *he* would be in terrible danger if the other Indians found out,' Cortes went on, 'and we owe him our lives.'

Topher could hardly wait to tell Naxos and his brothers the good news.

Chapter 17

Before they set off again Cortes made a rousing speech.

'Soon we shall have food in plenty. Meanwhile we have water, thanks to our Totonac friends!'

He lifted Naxos onto Doña Marina's grey mare, so that 'he' could ride behind her and told Topher that he and Ka could ride with him. But 'soon' wasn't the word. There were two more days without food, but on the third day they reached a town called Altatonga where the chief welcomed them with gifts of maize and eggs and turkey meat. On full stomachs the expedition made good speed. Soon the lake and salt marshes were behind them and the road turned west. They passed through several small towns in quick succession, where chiefs greeted them with all due ceremony, and then the road turned south. Now they were on the other side of the volcanic mountain – they could see its smoking summit – heading straight for Tlaxcala.

'So where are the Tlaxcalans?' said El Sol when they came to a high wall stretching from east to west for as far as they could see.

'On the other side of the wall?' said his brother, Gonzalez.

Quickly the telescope passed from one brigade leader to another. There was a ripple of unease. Why had no one warned them about this wall? It couldn't have been put up quickly, and the gate through it was narrow.

El Sol examined it and said, 'It's a trap. The gate doesn't go directly through the wall, which is twenty paces wide. It opens into a twisting passage wide enough for only two men at a time and only one on horseback. Let's go west.'

His brothers and several other commanders agreed with him. To the west was a range of mountains, which they would have to cross sometime. Why not here? It was a more direct route. There was a pass and they didn't need the Tlaxcalans who could be behind the wall waiting to attack them. But Doña Marina disagreed. She assured Cortes he could rely on Xicotencatl, the Tlaxcalan chief.

'The wall is to keep Montezuma and his armies out. It marks beginning of Tlaxcalan territory. Xicotencatl will be coming to meet us.'

So Cortes urged everyone forward.

It took hours for the whole company to pass through and it was mid afternoon before they were all in the field on the other side of the wall. Then they saw Tlaxcalans who appeared suddenly, stamping their feet and whooping and howling. As if by magic the green slope above the conquistadors turned red, then white, then red again, as hundreds, or even thousands of Indians swirled their red and white capes.

Cortes said, 'Topher, get the gifts for Xicotencatl from the saddlebags.' And as Topher slid off Diablo's back he heard his master call out, 'I thank you for your dance of welcome, and bring gifts and greetings!'

But Doña Marina, who Topher expected to translate his

words, said, 'My lord. That is not Xicotencatl the elder. It is his son.' She was looking through the telescope. 'That is not a dance of welcome. It is a dance of war.'

Xicotencatl the younger – if it was he – wore a cape of feathers and a helmet with a huge beak. Massed behind was an army of feathered warriors, their faces painted in red and white squares.

Cortes called out, 'Lay down your arms. We come as friends and allies!' as the front line leaped into the air, but Doña Marina was already turning her horse. 'My lord, it is too late for that. They do their start of battle dance.'

For a moment disbelief darkened Cortes' face, then he whirled round to face his men. 'TO ARMS! We attack while they're still dancing! Doña Marina, Topher, Ka get back behind the wall!'

Doña Marina kicked her mare into a gallop and headed for the gate.

Topher grabbed Ka's basket from Diablo's back – and saw that she wasn't inside! The door was open. As the ground throbbed with stamping feet and beating drums he scanned the field. Where was she? He heard Cortes cry, 'Horsemen, keep lances short and make for their eyes! Swordsmen, aim at their bowels.'

Then the conquistadors surged forward nearly knocking Topher off his feet.

Recovering his balance, just, he started to weave in and out of men who were grasping weapons and getting into fighting positions, but soon realised there was no chance of reaching the wall. It was like swimming against a ferocious tide. So he made for the side of the field, dodging between the fighting men who were surging forward, and managed to throw himself into a hollow behind a bush. But where was Ka? From his hidey-hole he could see ten conquistadors on horseback on the front line. Massed behind them were foot soldiers with crossbowmen behind them. Behind them Totonacs were pulling on padded armour – but before they were ready, before he could see if Nico and his brothers were among them – the front rank of Tlaxcalans surged forward.

'Follow the banner, the sign of the Holy Cross!'

Cortes led the Spanish cavalry into the fray. Six of them galloped straight at the oncoming Tlaxcalans, muskets firing, and Topher expected this to stop them in their tracks. Expected the Tlaxcalans to freeze with terror at the 'six-legged beasts' and 'firesticks'. But they didn't. They kept advancing and on the outer flank a horse fell, its throat slit, and another. Topher couldn't see whose. And the Tlaxcalans knocked down the standard bearer, and trampled over the holy cross.

Now some conquistadors were scared. Topher could see it in their eyes, heard them calling for priests to bless them before they died. For more and more Tlaxcalan warriors kept surging into the fray, whole lines of them. They didn't seem afraid of horses or firesticks or steel swords or anything. Another line was hurtling down the slope now, a wave of red and black, a perfect line, more like dancers than warriors, except that they hurled stones and spears at the conquistadors, and when they got in close, they struck them hard with clubs stuck with razors.

Then a noise like thunder – Topher ducked and

covered his ears – as a cannon ball hurtled overhead. Then another. And another. Surely the cannon would stop the Tlaxcalans? Cannon balls shattered their lines. Shattered the hillside. Earth and flesh flew into the air. Surely now they would retreat? But no. A third line rushed forward. Topher couldn't believe it, couldn't believe that the Tlaxcalans kept advancing though cannon balls were hurtling into them, blowing their bodies into bloody joints of meat. But some of them, hordes of them, were still getting through. And now a fourth line was sweeping down from the hill. And there were more lines behind them. The hillside was a chequerboard of red and white, and close to him bodies were falling, but all he could do was pray, for himself, for his cat and all his friends.

The battle went on till nightfall, but neither side surrendered. The Tlaxcalans retreated to their hill, but the conquistadors were trapped. They soon learned they were surrounded by Tlaxcalans and could not retreat beyond the wall. And early next morning a lookout said more Tlaxcalans were approaching, an army of fresh troops, perhaps five hundred strong, coming towards them from the west.

'Then we are done for,' said El Sol.

But Doña Marina asked for the telescope. Then she said, 'It is Xicotencatl the Elder and the troops he pledged to us.'

'But does he come as friend or foe?' said Cortes.

Chapter 18

Xicotencatl the Elder came as friend, or so he said. The battle had been a terrible mistake, he said, the result of a misunderstanding between father and son. The warriors who had fought for his son were not even Tlaxcalans. They were from the neighbouring Otomi tribe. He ordered them to lay down their arms and they obeyed him. He made his son apologise to Cortes on bended knees for taking up arms against him. He pledged his allegiance to Cortes and gestured towards the five hundred new arrivals.

'I bring you the Tlaxcalan warriors I pledged to you. They will ride with you to Tenochtitlan.'

And they did, though no one trusted them. And Xicotencatl the younger led them, though no one trusted him. They arrived at Tenochtitlan weeks later than they had planned, but just in time. It was the eighth day of November.

To Topher it seemed like a miracle that he and Ka had survived to see this day. Here they were on the southern shore of Lake Texcoco, and there in front of them was a causeway, wide enough for eight horses, and some five leagues long – and it led to the floating city so they didn't need to build boats. In the distance towers and turrets and the top of a white pyramid rose from the shimmering water. Were they real? Cortes, still mounted, looked through his telescope and seemed to think so. Doña Marina, by his side, was saying it was as she remembered. What did Naxos-Patti think? Topher tried to catch her eye, but she was staring straight ahead – at Doña Marina's back – as she had since the battle in which all her brothers had died. What was Cortes' plan now? Victory without Battle? That seemed unlikely. Attack first was the new motto and there had been many battles since Tlaxcala. Would he destroy Tenochtitlan, as he'd destroyed Cholula the last town they'd come through, or pretend to be the long-awaited god, Quetzalcoatl?

'It's a mirage,' he heard someone say.

'We are dreaming,' said someone else.

'Then you had better wake up,' said Cortes. 'For here, if I am not mistaken, is the man we have come to see. Four men dressed like that parrot, Teudile, are carrying some sort of litter. Others walk before them sweeping the ground with feathered fans, and people fall to the ground as it passes.' He handed the telescope to Doña Marina. 'Do you think that is Montezuma?'

Doña Marina thought it was. 'Quick, Topher, fetch your master's armour and the helmet which looks like Quetzalcoatl's for he must look godlike, grander than Montezuma and more powerful. Then you and Naxos both' – She shook Naxos-Patti's arm – 'put on your pages' livery and stand by your master with Ka.'

Cortes gave orders to his commanders.

'Gentleman, gird yourselves in battle gear and line up your troops. Get the Indians to put on their war paint and make a bit of noise, just in case Montezuma hasn't heard what we did at Cholula!'

They had left no one alive in Cholula. Cortes was hedging his bets.

By the time everyone was dressed and in position, the Aztec procession, though moving slowly, was closer. Now Topher could see the feathered litter, borne shoulder high, but it looked like a strange headless bird. Cortes in his best brocade doublet looked much more magnificent, and so did Doña Marina in her flowing red cape, and so did he and Naxos-Patti in their pages' outfits.

'See the crossroads ahead where a canal meets this!' Cortes called out. 'We'll head for that and then stop with the sign of the cross held high! There's a building there so be prepared for an ambush!'

Two priests with silver crosses took their places beside Cortes mounted on Diablo. In front of them were four more horsemen in full armour. Then came Cristobal de Corres twisting and twirling the flag of Castile, so that it fluttered and flew like a bird.

'Don't even think of it, Ka.'

Sometimes she leaped at the flag, but today she stood by Topher, as if she were taking seriously her role as Ocelotl. Ever since she'd come back after the battle with the Tlaxcalans even Cortes trusted her not to run away. Now horses pawed the ground, eager to be off, and harness jingled. Glancing over his shoulder, Topher saw a contingent of infantry with drawn swords, then more horsemen with lances, then crossbowmen, quivers at their sides, and hundreds of Indians dressed and painted for war. He could hear their whooping as they struck their hands against their mouths. Then as Cortes cried, 'Forward we go for God and King and holy saints!' they were off to the sound of drums.

Soon Topher could see the front of the litter sparkling with jewels, and the chequered faces of the four men carrying it. Two more men carried the yellow-feathered canopy and six more walked before it, sweeping the road with feathered fans. Flute players and drummers marched behind them, and behind them, came whirling dancers. Closer and closer they got then, as they reached the crossroads, both companies came to a halt beneath the walls of a tall red brick building and there was silence.

For several minutes both sides were still. Then two of the fan-bearing Aztecs put down their fans, stepped towards the litter with averted eyes and drew back a curtain. Now the litter framed a small hook-nosed man in a huge feathered headdress.

'Art thou Montezuma?' said Cortes, ignoring the fan-bearing Aztecs gesturing frantically to him. 'Art thou he?'

Doña Marina translated, and the man replied, 'I am he and I bow down before you and I bid you welcome for this is your home.'

In fact he didn't bow down, but he did step out of the litter, and as he did a long embroidered cloak settled in a pool round his sandalled feet.

Cortes must have been pleased at his words, but he showed no emotion as he dismounted. Then ignoring the gasps and gesticulations of the bearers he stepped forward saying, 'Fear not, Montezuma, for we love you

110

greatly.' And he put a pearl necklace round his neck.

Naxos-Patti gasped, 'It is forbidden to touch the emperor.' But Montezuma made no objection. Instead he gestured to one of the shocked bearers, who approached Cortes and put two necklaces round his neck. One was of red snail shells, the other of gold shrimps.

Topher couldn't take his eyes off Montezuma. By now he was used to faces studded with stones and jewels, but the emperor's jewels were bigger than any he'd seen before. From his nose hung a heavy gold and turquoise ring. More gold pieces plugged his ears and there was a white stone in his lower lip inlaid with blue, shaped like a humming bird. What was he thinking? It was impossible to see. Did he really think Cortes was Quetzalcoatl? For several moments he looked searchingly at him – and at Ka. Then he said, 'O lords, you must be tired for you have come a long way, but you have arrived at your home. Follow me and I will take you to your dwelling place.'

When Doña Marina translated this, there were murmurs of relief from the conquistadors. The man had said 'your home' twice! Could Cortes' audacious plan be working? Then this was going to be easier than everyone anticipated!

But Ka didn't think so. She didn't want to follow Montezuma. As he got back into his litter, she leaped into Topher's arms. As Cristobal de Corres began to twirl the banner and Cortes urged his horse forward, she dug her claws into Topher's sleeve. When he started to walk beside Cortes – for what else could he do? – she growled.

Trrra...p. Trrra...p.

He was glad he was wearing his thick Spanish doublet.

Trrra...p. Trrra...p.

'I'm sorry, Ka, but I can't disobey my master.'

But surely she was right to be fearful, for the long causeway to the island city was made of wooden sections. The Aztecs could remove some once they had them in the city. And what might they do then, or even before? The water beside the causeway was full of canoes, packed with Aztecs. At any moment they could leap onto the conquistadors and slit their throats with their sharp little knives. Fewer than two hundred conquistadors had survived the journey. Over fifty had died, many of them in the battle with the Tlaxcalans. Before them were thousands of Aztecs and behind them were five hundred Tlaxcalans, led by a man who only two weeks ago had been their deadly enemy.

Chapter 19

For the time being though, Montezuma seemed determined to treat Cortes as an honoured guest. His subjects, lining the causeway, waved feathers not knives, and when the procession entered the city, more feather-waving crowds lined the streets and canals, cheering as the visitors passed, and even more lay on flat rooftops showering them with perfumed petals. There were flowers everywhere, growing in gardens, trailing from baskets, floating in water. It was the most beautiful city Topher had ever seen, dominated by the white pyramid in the centre. As they got closer, the pyramid seemed to get larger, and the scent of petals couldn't disguise a more sinister smell. Then they were standing in a huge square, and they saw the cause of the stench. A double row of steps leading to the top of the pyramid was thick with dry and drying blood.

Montezuma stepped out of the litter. Was this the moment when he ordered them to be sacrificed? Was this the moment when his warriors attacked? Black-clad priests, looking like vultures, bordered the steps. Rows of white skulls glistened in the sunlight.

'Gracious lords!'

To Topher's relief, Montezuma was pointing away from the pyramid, drawing their attention to a building on the east side of the square. 'Welcome to your home, the Palace of Axayacatl. Please rest now after the hardships of your journey.'

Doña Marina translated his words. She also told Cortes that the Palace of Axayacatl had belonged to Montezuma's father. Montezuma lived in a bigger palace on the south side of the square. Cortes glanced at the larger one for a moment, but then followed the Aztec chief through an archway into a courtyard, where he dismounted.

Ka growled. *Trrrap. Trrrap.*

But Cortes and Doña Marina followed the chief up a stone staircase into the building – and so did Topher. The room they entered was richly furnished. Topher had never seen anything like it, but the chief swept through it into another room, and then another, and then another, each more richly furnished than the last, till they came to one with a dais at the end and two ornate thrones. Montezuma sat on one throne and patted the other.

'Sit, gracious lord!'

Cortes sat – and a huge eagle made of gold looked down on him. Topher could hardly believe what he saw. The Indians didn't have furniture! That's what he thought. But these Aztecs did. They had everything, except doors.

'Why not?' Cortes asked.

'We don't need them,' Montezuma replied. 'In Tenochtitlan no one steals.'

Now bearers brought in gifts for Cortes. They put garlands of flowers round his neck. They tipped bags of jewels and golden figurines and cocoa beans at his feet. They put a feather cloak round his shoulders. Then six of them carried in a cartwheel made of gold, and at last Cortes smiled – and he sent for Yanez the carpenter to build him a stronghold.

'Tell him I may need to lock up a few people as well, so he'd better find wood for some doors.'

That night, Topher and Naxos-Patti slept outside their master and mistress's bedchamber, where Cortes and Doña Marina slept on a gilded bed, piled high with soft mattresses and pillows. But next morning Cortes woke early and sent Topher to rouse the other conquistadors.

'Tell them to meet me in front of the pyramid in half an hour. We are going on a sightseeing tour!'

It began at the town square where slaves were busy sweeping the ground and polishing statues. When Father Merced arrived holding a crucifix, Cortes pointed to the thatched building at the top of the pyramid. 'The sooner we claim that for Christ the better. Some of their priests are up there, but there's enough of us to deal with them.'

About twenty conquistadors had answered his summons, but more were on their way.

'Follow me, gentlemen!' Cortes unsheathed his sword and started to climb. The others followed – and the Aztec priests descended like a flock of crows.

Cortes called out, 'I am Quetzalcoatl and I say make way for a greater God!'

But the priests took no notice. Jeronimo translated, but they still ignored him. More and more of them appeared, from all parts of the pyramid. Then they perched, about sixty of them, just six steps above the

115

conquistadors, spreading their arms as if they thought they could stop the trespassers.

But Cortes acted as if they were not there. Several priests went tumbling as the conquistadors pushed them aside. Topher, holding Cortes' telescope, was puffing, but Cortes kept climbing till they were about halfway up, when he paused to survey the scene below.

The square was full of open-mouthed Indians, and Montezuma had arrived. He was standing in front of his litter, surrounded by priests and attendants. Suddenly his attendants began to climb the steps – he must have ordered them – but conquistadors pulled them back. More conquistadors were coming out of the Palace of Axayacatl.

'Good,' said Cortes. 'And they're bringing our holy statues. Let us go and make room for them.'

The last bit of the climb was the hardest. The smell was disgusting. Topher didn't want to breathe, but couldn't not breathe. He was puffing. They were all puffing. Then, at last they were at the top, on the platform, standing before some sort of curtained shrine which hummed.

'Shall I do the honours?' said Cortes.

As he swept back the curtain a cloud of flies flew out engulfing them. It was several minutes before Topher dare open his eyes. Then he saw what he'd glimpsed before, two goggle-eyed statues, crusty with dry blood, garlanded with freshly-skinned human heads. The statues stood at the ends of a table, where a pan of human hearts stood steaming.

'And look who's coming,' said Cortes as they heard a clatter behind them.

It was Montezuma himself, in his litter. Before him came armed warriors and an Aztec priest bearing a wooden staff.

Cortes waited silently, till the grim party was close. Then he seized the priest's staff and attacked the idols in the shrine, leaping up to beat their heads, so that the blood fell off in huge red-black scabs.

Warriors, priest and Montezuma watched in silence, as if they expected Cortes to be struck down dead by the angry gods. But nothing happened and Cortes cried, 'See, your gods are only stone! Now you must believe in our God who made heaven and earth. By his works you will know who the master is!'

By midday all the pagan statues had gone from the pyramid, and the statues of Jesus Christ and the Holy Mother Mary and Saint Christopher stood on top. In the afternoon Father Sahagun celebrated the Christian mass. Soon afterwards a group of Aztecs arrived at the bottom of the steps with a bunch of wilting maize stalks.

'Can the Christian god make it rain?' they asked.

'If you believe in him,' said Father Sahagun.

Next day it rained and hundreds of Aztecs swarmed to the square saying they wanted to become Christians. Montezuma swore allegiance to the King of Spain. Topher could hardly believe it. Cortes had achieved victory without battle.

The following days seemed too good to be true. When they had finished their chores, Topher and Naxos-Patti explored Tenochtitlan, rejoicing that they didn't have to go to strict schools like Aztec children. One day they went with Cortes and Doña Marina to the wondrous House of Birds, where birds like jewels flew in and out of trees and trellises, brilliant with flowers. They had glimpsed it from the palace windows, but only when they were inside could they walk through the gardens on jade pathways, or dip their fingers in sparking waterfalls. Only when they were inside could they enter the Totocalli, the treasure house where Montezuma kept his most precious jewels. Not that they remained there for long, for as soon as Cortes saw them, he claimed them for himself. Soon he had rooms – with locked doors – full of gold and jewels, and he seemed content, till one hot afternoon in April when the conquistadors were resting in the courtyard of the Palace of Axayacatl.

A dry stillness filled the air because it hadn't rained for weeks. Even Ka, who loved warmth, sought the shade of the kapok tree, whose fluffy seeds she sometimes batted. But today she slept and so did Topher, when suddenly the peace was shattered by the sound of clattering hooves, and a dust-coated conquistador galloped into the courtyard.

Ordered to dismount by Cortes, he undid a bloody saddlebag and out rolled a severed head with a curly black beard.

'Arguello!' Someone recognised one of the conquistadors left in Veracruz.

'It is he!' gasped the man, who said he'd galloped from Veracruz with an urgent message from the sheriff.

'Governor General Cortes, I beg you, return immediately to Veracruz, for it is under double attack! From

Aztecs, who have been plotting against you, while seeming to pay you allegiance, and from your old enemy, the Governor of Cuba. He has sent an armada to arrest you for rebelling against the crown. He says if you do not return immediately to Veracruz and swear allegiance to the King of Spain and hand over all the gold you have acquired, he will order his men to kill every single conquistador in the town.'

'But I have sworn allegiance to the King,' said Cortes. 'I have sent him a letter, promising him the riches I find here. And I have left a copy of that letter with the Sheriff of Veracruz.'

'Well, the Governor has seen no such letter, and he says he will raze Veracruz to the ground if you do not return!'

El Sol said, 'Perhaps the letter got lost, Capitan General?'

'Then I must return to Veracruz to save my people and defend my good name!' Cortes turned to El Sol. 'Arrest Montezuma and charge him with treason. You will be in charge while I am gone! De Sandeval, prepare to leave for the coast with one hundred men to go to the aid of de Escalante! ' And with that he swept from the room.

Looking down, Topher saw his own hands trembling.

Looking up, he saw El Sol smiling.

Chapter 20

Was this what El Sol wanted all along? Had he planned to replace Cortes? Had he hoped that the Governor of Cuba would attack so that Cortes would have to return to Veracruz, leaving him in charge?

As Cortes and Doña Marina galloped out of the courtyard next day, Topher felt sick, for they would not take him with them.

'Stop sulking, boy!' El Sol stood on the palace steps. 'Find your little friend, and start moving my belongings into the Governor General's quarters!' Then he laughed as something else caught his eye – his brothers coming into the courtyard. 'Goodness gracious! Someone else is moving into his new quarters, and my kind brothers are helping him!'

Gomez and Gonzalez each held the end of a chain. Gonzalez called out, 'Where do you want him, Governor General?'

El Sol replied, 'In the Eagle Room!'

'Come on, dog!' As Gomez yanked the chain, Montezuma fell sprawling.

Topher didn't wait to see more. He went to find Naxos-Patti, but they saw the Aztec chief later, chained to the throne in the Eagle Room. El Sol was holding a gold mask. 'This is very pretty, o great leader, but have you remembered where the gold comes from yet? Or do

120

you like wearing those chains?'

'Where are the mines?' Gonzalez pressed his face to the emperor's. 'Where are the panning fields?'

'Tell us and we'll unchain you,' said El Sol and Montezuma told them of a river in the northern territory where gold flowed freely.

Later they heard El Sol sending one of his brothers and another conquistador to find it, but he kept Montezuma in chains. He had heard that trouble was brewing, and it was, *because* Montezuma was in chains.

Word soon got round, for the emperor had many visitors who were horrified when they saw him. Priests with matted hair and slashed earlobes turned away their faces. Nobles in full regalia hung their heads, not because they felt unworthy to look, but because they could not bear to see his shame.

'Big trouble coming,' Naxos-Patti whispered to Topher. 'Priests soon get new leader.'

'But surely they can't?'

'Yes,' she said. 'They can. You do not understand. Montezuma is only highest in the land *while the priests said so*. They choose new leader easily, and now they think time good for change. Soon Aztec new year begin. Last year, Year of Reed, bad for kings. This year, Year of Flint, good. So now good time to rise against foreign devils and false Christian god. Must hold festival for Tlaloc, rain god.'

She looked worried. 'Tlaloc demands many child sacrifice.'

Topher tried to reassure her. 'Cortes has forbade them to worship their gods. El Sol will not allow it.'

121

But El Sol was in charge now and he did. He soon heard that the Aztecs wanted to replace Montezuma with a strong ruler, who would rise up against the Spanish, and let them worship their own gods. So he let Montezuma tell the priests that the Rain Festival could take place.

Next day Topher and Naxos-Patti saw the horrible goggle-eyed statues that Cortes had attacked, on the top of the pyramid. They were next to Saint Christopher and the Virgin Mary and Jesus Christ. When Naxos-Patti saw them, she was terrified. Crowds had begun to gather in the square, and two Aztec priests appeared on the steps of the pyramid with a red and yellow bag.

'That is for sacrifice to Tlaloc. Names of children go in bag. Priests pick out victims. Some are drowned. Some have hearts cut out.'

Topher prayed for Cortes to return quickly, but more bad news had arrived that morning. A messenger brought Montezuma a letter from one of his spies at the coast. It didn't reach him of course. El Sol got to it first and it wasn't hard to read, for it was a picture showing eighteen ships arriving at Veracruz, all full of armed men. El Sol had shown it to his brothers.

'The Cuban Governor must have sent over nine hundred fighting men to take Cortes dead or alive! I fear I may have to stay in the Governor General's quarters.'

Now Topher felt sick with guilt. If he had delivered the letter to de Escalante this wouldn't have happened. The priests started to walk among the crowd with the red and yellow bag. Naxos-Patti said they were asking for the names of victims to be written on stones and placed in the bag. What if El Sol put hers in? Then Topher had a more positive thought. What if it wasn't too late to help Cortes – and Naxos-Patti? What if El Sol still had the letter? Might he have kept it safe, to keep his options open? Then it would be among his possessions. Surely it was worth trying to find it, and if they did, couldn't they take it to Cortes?

They hurried back to the palace. Naxos-Patti was keen to start looking.

'We find letter, then we leave tonight by quick road. I know quick road. Everyone know, except Cortes when we came by long route.'

Fortunately, when they got back El Sol told them to hurry up and finish moving his belongings into Cortes' rooms, so they started looking straightaway.

Chapter 21

They soon found the letter at the bottom of a box where El Sol kept his private papers. But then Topher hesitated. Should he take it now or later? What if El Sol checked the box and discovered the scroll was missing before nightfall?

'Take now,' said Naxos-Patti. 'Hard to take later.'

That was true. He kept the box under his bed. It would be risky sneaking in there while he was sleeping.

'But if El Sol discovers it has gone he will search us.'

'Then I hide it,' said Naxos-Patti. 'Outside, to pick up later, when I go to market.'

The Aztecs had stopped delivering food to the palace. Some market traders would not sell to Spaniards. The cook thought Naxos, as he thought she was, would have a better chance of buying food as he was an Indian. So 'he' put on his native dress and hid the scroll under the cape. When 'he' came back, with bread and eggs, 'he' said he'd hidden it behind a statue, near the gate by the northern causeway.

But 'he' was nervous. There was still talk of rebellion in the town, after the festival, and Aztecs were busy choosing names and writing them on stones to go in the red and yellow bag. Worse, one of her brother's friends, a Totonac boy called Quexos, had given 'him' a funny look.

'Would he betray you to the priests?'

'If he think I to blame for trouble.'

Luckily El Sol didn't pay them much attention for the rest of the day, and by nightfall they had carried all his property to the Governor General's quarters. Now they hoped he would go to his bedchamber early, or fall asleep at the dining table, as he often did when he had drunk too much. But he and his brothers were in party mood. Many conquistadors came to dine with them, and Topher and Naxos-Patti were kept busy waiting at table. They kept filling everyone's goblets as soon as they were empty, but instead of getting sleepy, people got livelier. Someone called for playing cards. Another called for musicians and when Benito the tambourine man arrived, some of them began to dance. Topher yawned, deliberately, as he filled El Sol's glass yet again. Wasn't yawning catching? But his new master laughed. 'Do you want to go to bed with your little girlfriend?'

Everyone heard him. He spoke in one of those silences that sometimes happen for no particular reason. Everyone had stopped talking. The musicians were between tunes.

El Sol laughed at their open mouths. 'Oh, don't you know about Topher's secret girlfriend?'

Patti was out of the room, fetching more wine, and Topher hoped, without much hope, that El Sol would say no more, but he did.

'Maybe I should say boyfriend? Because he or she keeps changing! Perhaps the little witch cat casts spells? Oh yes, Topher has secrets and he can be careless! So I

125

must watch him carefully. If Captain Cortes knew how careless he would be very cross. But luckily for him I don't think Captain Cortes will be coming back.'

His brothers laughed.

Cortes' chamberlain and major-domo looked alarmed and El Sol laughed at them. 'Oh, you two need not worry. You won't be without a job for Cortes made me his legal successor. Oh yes. He said so, he *wrote* so before he left. You don't believe me? Fetch me my box of private papers, Topher!'

Topher froze.

El Sol shouted, 'Fetch me my private papers!'

'Y-yes, Capitan de Alvarado.'

'*Governor General* de Alvarado!'

Topher shot to the door with El Sol's voice ringing in his ears, and nearly ran into Patti, coming in with a flagon of wine.

'We must leave now.' He spoke in Nahuatl hoping no one present could understand.

She hesitated – and El Sol saw her. He turned towards the others. 'You don't believe she's a girl? Wait a minute and I'll show you!'

Patti obviously hadn't understood because she stepped into the room, and tripped over Ka, who obviously had. As Ka ran in front of her, Patti fell headlong and the wine went flying.

She picked herself up and headed for the kitchen saying, 'I get more!'

'And I get cloth!' said Topher.

They conferred in the kitchen doorway.

'What now?' said Topher. 'Get the box and run? Or run?'

'Run,' said Patti. 'He so drunk he forget.'

'No such luck. Listen.'

'TOPHER, THE BOX PRONTO! AND YOU, GIRL, MORE WINE!'

Patti called out, 'I get more!' But she didn't.

Topher raced upstairs, got the box and came down with it. Then he took it into El Sol – and yawned again. But El Sol laughed nastily. 'You can go to bed when your little friend has brought us more wine. Tell her to hurry.'

But Topher didn't tell her. Of course not. He told one of the other servants to take El Sol more wine and went straight to the kitchen door where she was waiting with Ka.

They'd planned their escape carefully, but for later when everyone else was asleep. But now it was too risky to wait. They had to go now, hoping no one would stop them. A cook was sitting on the step smoking his clay pipe. Other servants were under a tree in the middle of the courtyard, playing patolli. Luckily none of them took much notice, even when Patti opened a gate in the wall and walked through it, into another courtyard.

Ka leaped ahead of them, checking that each courtyard was safe, before signalling with a flick of her head that they should follow. And as they ran from one courtyard to another, Topher hoped the guards on the outer gate would believe their stories – that Naxos had permission to join his family for the festival, and he had to deliver a bread order to the bakers. Now they could hear a noise of music and shouting from the Dance House just south of the palace. Good. The gateway was just opposite. They reached it. Not so good. It was blocked by guards who were trying to keep out a crowd of Aztecs who said they wanted to rescue Montezuma. A musket went off. The crowd fell back, but more guards appeared. A scuffle broke out, blocking the gateway, and the guards didn't notice their cries or their hands tugging at their clothes.

Or they took no notice. Topher looked behind them, scared he might see someone coming to see why a shot had been fired. Scared that El Sol himself might have discovered the scroll was missing. Shouts came from the direction of the kitchen.

'TOPHER!'

And Ka had gone. Where was she?

'Mi-aaw!' She was at his feet. *This way!* She ran back to the courtyard they'd just come through. But why?

He saw why. 'Patti, come on!' There was a tree in the corner near the outer wall and Ka was halfway up it. They followed her up the tree. Then they clung together as El Sol and his brothers ran into the yard with unsheathed swords. They held their breath as the men kept running – into the next courtyard, yelling, 'Have you seen two brats?' And Topher and Patti dropped out of the tree into the street below.

The crowd at the gate had grown bigger and noisier. People were pouring out of the Dance House. They heard El Sol again. 'Have you seen two brats and a cat?' But they didn't wait to hear more. They sped north, keeping in the shadows close to the palace wall. They heard El Sol shouting orders of some kind. Then there was another explosion and all went quiet. All they could hear then was their own footsteps, the sound of lapping water and canoes knocking against each other, for they'd reached the main street with waterways on either side. They ran past houses, hoping all the inhabitants were fast asleep. They passed burning braziers at each street corner, but when they reached the Great Market they slowed down, partly because they were out of breath, partly because running was not a good idea. They were getting close to the main gate where guards would be on the lookout.

Their plan was to retrieve the scroll from behind the statue of Huitzilopochtli where Patti had hidden it, then lie low, beneath a market stall perhaps, till dawn when the gates would be opened for traders to pass to and fro. Somehow they would slip through with the crowds and get onto the mainland.

It took them a while to find the right statue because there were several and they all looked the same in the dark, but at last Patti found the scroll. She had it in her hand, when they heard a sneering voice.

'And what do you plan to do with that?' It was El Sol, and he had his hands round Ka's neck.

His brothers were with him. Gonzalez twisted Topher's arm behind his back.

Gomez grabbed Patti. 'Don't move, unless you want to eat your friend for dinner.'

'As for you, Witch Cat,' El Sol addressed Ka, who

dangled in front of his face, 'you might still be...
OWEEEE!'

He howled as Ka flipped over, scratching his face
with her hind claws – she seemed to do a backward
somersault in the air – and *dissolve*. Or that's what it
seemed to Topher, who couldn't see well with a knife
against his throat.

'March!' said Gonzalez. 'And don't you try any tricks!'

Chapter 22

'What do we do now?' Topher's voice was gloomy and Patti didn't answer. They were prisoners in a small room, high up in the Palace of Axayacatl.

'Look,' Patti sounded frightened as she peered out of a tiny window onto the square below. 'God of War on pyramid now.'

They could see the top of the pyramid clearly. It was crowded with statues, not just Tlaloc the rain god but others, and the biggest was the war god, Huitzilopochtli. Sunlight bounced off his pointed gold nose and the gold serpents hanging from his ears.

'He wear battle cloak of nettles and bones,' said Patti. 'And he carry arrows.'

There were priests at the top with flaming torches, purifying the platform for more sacrifices, Patti said. She expected El Sol to come for her at any moment, to try and appease the angry Aztecs. Best not to think about that.

Topher said, 'I wonder where Ka is.'

Patti said, 'She fine. She hunt and feed. We starve.'

They had not eaten all day. Nor had anyone in the palace. They knew this because they'd heard the guards outside grumbling. Starving the Spanish was official Aztec policy. In the square below, Aztecs were hammering a circle of tall stakes into the ground.

'What are those stakes for? Is that part of the ritual?'

Patti shook her head. 'Stakes new, and so are big pots, but listen, guards back.'

There were two of them – called Eduardo and Rodrigues – and they'd been to look for food. They sounded frightened. They had heard the rumours that the Aztecs were planning to attack as soon as their festival was over.

'No chance,' said Rodrigues. 'A hundred of us, thousands of them.'

'And the stakes are for us,' said Eduardo. 'They're going to kill us and cook us in those pots. They say the tallest one's for El Sol.'

'Why doesn't he release Montezuma and tell him to call off the rebellion?'

'Because the Tlaxcalans say the Aztecs would see that as a sign to attack.'

'And nobody obey Montezuma now,' said Patti. 'He humiliated.'

Topher couldn't help thinking of Ka. *Trrr...ap. Trrr...aap*, she'd warned, even before they'd set foot on Tenochtitlan. Where was she now?

'Listen.' Patti nudged him. 'Someone else outside.'

They heard the name Hernan and Topher's heart leaped. That was his master's Christian name.

Patti shook her head. 'It Hernan of Texcoca tribe. He become Christian and take new leader's name. Listen. He sound terrified.'

She was right. He was gibbering. The Aztecs were about to scale the walls of the palace with ladders. The Aztecs were boring holes in the rear walls, to set fire to the building. They were all sure to die.

132

Eduardo and Rodrigues began to argue.

Eduardo wanted to leave straightaway.

Rodrigues said if they did El Sol would kill them for disobeying orders.

Eduardo said, 'Wouldn't he rather we killed Aztecs than guard a couple of brats?'

Then someone else arrived. 'Orders from El Sol! Get out! Hide yourselves on east side entrance of square. As soon as they're all in we're going to attack, before they attack us. Quick! There's no time to waste. It's them or us. They've started pulling up drawbridges and ripping up causeways to stop us leaving!'

Trap. Trap. Ka was right.

'Let us out first!' Topher and Patti shouted.

But no one answered. They heard swords leaving sheaths.

'At least put the cord through the latchhole so we can let ourselves out!' Topher yelled desperately. 'Or raise the bar before you go!'

No answer.

They heard feet pounding down the stone stairs, heard them getting fainter and fainter.

They hammered on the door. They made themselves hoarse with shouting, but all three had gone. It seemed as if everyone had gone. Or was Montezuma still downstairs, chained to the throne in the Eagle room? They had no means of knowing. They were alone in an upper room, and the door was barred.

Chapter 23

Stretching on tiptoe, Topher managed to peer through the latchhole, but he couldn't see if the cord was dangling or not. The cord was attached to the bar. If it was still there he might be able to draw it through the hole and lift the bar out of its socket. But all he could see was the red wall opposite the door. He looked round for something long and flexible – to hook round the cord and pull it through – but the room was bare.

It was one of the strongholds Cortes used for keeping prisoners.

'Have you got a knife? El Sol took mine.'

She shook her head. He'd taken hers too. They couldn't even whittle away a piece of the floor or door and fashion it to the right shape. El Sol had made sure of that.

Patti was examining the window, their only other means of escape.

'No ladder. But if we had some of that we maybe get out.'

'Some of what?'

She pointed to the platform on top of the pyramid where four men were climbing up a post. The men wore wings and were heading for a little platform round the top of the post where ropes were dangling.

'Special rope,' said Patti. 'Made of rubber.'

The men were tying them round their middles. Then

suddenly they all leaped away from the pole, each in a different direction, and started to swing round it in a bouncy sort of flight.

'Each one go round thirteen times,' said Patti as the birdmen 'flew' round and round. 'To make lucky number fifty-two so sun god keep flying in sky. *They* believe,' she added quickly.

'Well it's better than sacrificing.'

'They do that after,' she replied. 'Many Aztecs come to see. Look.'

The square was nearly full with Aztecs, and Tlaxcalans, Topher thought. And conquistadors were getting into position at the four gateways. Where were the Christian priests? He couldn't see any, but could see El Sol and a conquistador called de Aguilar surveying everything from halfway up the pyramid steps.

El Sol's voice floated up to them. 'Welcome! Welcome! Enjoy your festival!'

But the Aztecs didn't take much notice. They were busy looking at the rotating birdmen.

'After birdmen, serpent dance, then sacrifice,' said Patti, as Topher went back to the door to have another go at peering through the latchhole. He still couldn't see the cord. Had their guards cut it off before they left?

'Window too small,' said Patti, trying to push her head through. She gave up and buried her head in her hands. 'No good. We die.'

'*Don't* say that! Don't think it. Look, the dance has started.'

The sound of drums and whining flutes floated through

135

the window as the square became a kaleidoscope of colours. Patterns of turquoise, green and red changed to red and white and yellow and then back again as a long line of feathered dancers coiled and uncoiled, swaying like a serpent to the beat of the drums. Above them, on the pyramid steps, an old man drummer banged with both hands. Above him stood El Sol and de Aguilar. A circle of drummers sat in the middle of the square, dancers whirling round them. And round them, thousands of Aztecs clapped and swayed to the hypnotic beat. Then . . . ATTACK! El Sol swirled his sword and the old man drummer's hands flew through the air.

Now conquistadors leaped from each of the four gateways, slicing through the dancers with their swords of steel. The music stopped. The dancers stopped and for several moments the only movement was of conquistadors moving through the crowd and Aztecs falling. The only sound was screaming. Then the Aztecs began to fight back. Tlaxcalans too, they were fighting, but on whose side Topher couldn't be sure. Everyone was fighting or trying to flee. But they couldn't flee for all the exits were blocked. Horrible, horrible screams filled the air. He could hear them even when he put his hands over his ears, even when he buried his head between his knees, and crouched in the corner beside Patti. And it went on for hours. The massacre went on for hours filling the room with the smell of blood and guts and emptying bowels.

But at last it went quiet outside, and inside. All Topher could hear was Patti's breathing. Then it stopped and he wondered if she had died of despair, but when he opened his eyes she was sitting up, alert. 'Can you hear that?'

'What?'

'Noise.' She nodded towards the door.

It was several moments before Topher could hear it – for the last few hours he'd been trying to cut out all sound – but then he heard a light knocking sound.

'We call out?' said Patti.

He shook his head. 'It might be an Aztec.'

'It might be Spanish – and we no get out we die.'

She was right. They were desperate for food and water. He said, 'You speak first – in Nahuatl. Ask who's there.'

She did – and there was no answer.

She tried again. Still no answer.

'You now.'

He waited. There it was again: a light, regular knocking. Then he said, 'Who goes there?' And there was a reply, 'Mw-ow-ow!'

Ka!

Topher shot to the door and peered through the latch-hole but saw nothing, not even the red wall. Darkness, that was all. But it wasn't dark yet, not outside. She must be blocking the hole.

'Ka. *Ka!* What are you doing?' She must be sitting or lying on the bar.

'Mwow-ow!' *Hole. Hole.*

'You're trying to get the cord into the hole?' He pictured it, Ka trying to catch hold of the cord, and draw it up. Ka dropping it. The knocking must be the knot on the end of the rope banging against the door.

'Keep trying, Ka!'

Don't wo ... rry. Don't wo ... rry. She was purring.

Then the purring stopped and he saw red through the hole. Oh no. She'd gone!

But then he saw her paw, her beautiful golden paw with cutlass claws gripping the knot of the cord. She'd got it to the other side of the hole, and was trying to push it through. It came closer, closer.

'Let me help.' He poked his fingers through the hole and managed to get hold of it. Pulled it. Felt it detach from her claws.

'Thank you, Ka. Thank you. Thank you.' He drew the cord into the room. He and Patti pulled on it together. They heard the creak of the bar rising. Then they put their weight against the door and pushed. And there was Ka!

She rubbed round his legs, briefly. Then 'Mwow-ow!' *Follow me!*

'Where are we going?'

You'll see. You'll see. No time to talk.

She sped down the first flight of stairs, tail erect. Waited at the bottom for them, looking up at them with wide golden eyes.

Hu ... rrry! Hu ... rrry!

But they couldn't run as fast as her. They were too weak.

'We need food, Ka, and water.'

Of cou ... rrr ... se. Of cou ... rrr ... se.

She led them down more stairs, through empty rooms, where there wasn't a crumb to be seen. They reached the kitchen on the ground floor, where the pump handle lay broken on the floor. No water there! On raced Ka, out of the kitchen into a courtyard, out of a gate, into another courtyard, through another gate. Suddenly it went dark and now they noticed the noise, the squawking and screeching and chattering. They must be close to the Bird Gardens where birds were settling for the night.

'Clever Ka,' said Patti. 'Food there and water.'

And wild animals, thought Topher, as Ka led them in, but these were desperate times. As they crept inside he hoped they were safely in their cages, and that someone had found time to feed them.

Chapter 24

Even in the dark Patti managed to find a tree bearing food.

'Eat,' she whispered as she handed Topher half of an egg-shaped fruit. 'Ahuacatl.'

'Isn't that what you wash with?'

'Food too. Good. Eat soft inside, not skin or big seed.'

It wasn't bad, and he was so hungry he would have eaten grass. Its creamy flesh slipped down his throat. They were sitting by a fountain and as Ka lapped at the water, he remembered the day they'd first come here. He'd wondered if Paradise might be like this, but now, in the dark, it seemed more sinister. He could hear the growls and barks of animals in cages and wondered where their keepers were.

'Here.' Patti handed him something that crunched when he bit into it. 'Corn cob. Better cooked but not bad. Tomorrow we set off for Veracruz to find Doña Marina and Cortes, but now we sleep. Yes?'

He wondered if he was already asleep having a beautiful dream – after the nightmare of the afternoon. White cup-shaped flowers seemed to shine out of the darkness. They filled his nose with a heady scent and drowned the memory of those other smells.

Patti shook his arm. 'Sleep now? Up high. Safer.' She'd started to climb a tree with palm-like leaves.

'Ka?' He touched her ears and she turned to look at him, her eyes large like twin moons. Then she followed Patti up the tree, nearly to the top, where the girl was sitting on a leaf which bounced with her weight. 'Sorry, no hammock, but leaves good.'

He found another leaf bigger than a hammock and lay down. Ka settled in the curl of his stomach. She began to purr; the leaf rocked; the wind whispered and in a few minutes he was asleep, dreaming of a shining bird with a long red tail.

'Ch...ap! Chap!' A sound like a pair of clapping hands woke him.

Ka was already awake, gazing at the end of the leaf where a green bird with a red breast and a golden crest shone from the darkness.

'Ch...ap. Chap.' A sort of chirp. Its yellow beak opened and closed.

Patti looked down from the leaf above. 'Quetzal!' She breathed the word. 'Messenger from Quetzalcoatl! Magic bird. Make wind blow.'

And the wind did blow, shaking the tree as the bird turned round and turned its back on Topher, spreading its tail before him like a shimmering carpet up a flight of stairs. This quetzal was huge, much much bigger than the one he'd seen before.

'Chap chap.' It looked over its shoulder. *Get on. Get on.*

Ka ran up the shimmering tail, right to the top, where she turned and looked down at him. 'Mwow! Mwow!' *Get on, Topher. Get on.*

Patti looked down from the leaf above, brown eyes shining. 'Get on, Topher.'

He looked up. 'You too. You must come.'

She laughed. 'Me too big. I go find mother and father in Veracruz. Quetzal take you find yours, but take this.' She dropped something down, a ball, a slippery ball, but he managed to catch it, though the leaf beneath him was shaking.

'Ch . . . ap. Ch . . . ap.' The bird was lifting one claw and then the other, flexing its feet as if impatient to be off. Then it moved its tail up and down, tickling his face and legs with its feathers – and he realised that he was tiny! A magic bird, yes! Patti was right and he must do as he was bid. So he started to climb, up and up the springy feathers, holding on with one hand, till he reached the top. Then up went the bird's tail sliding him into the hollow of its back where Ka was waiting. He knelt down. She settled between his knees. He tucked the ball inside his doublet, and put his arms round the bird's strong neck as it turned and walked backwards along the leaf towards the edge of the tree, and before he had time to say *Adios* to Patti, it stepped off the leaf. They were falling! He clung on, elbows holding Ka, but then, wings flapping furiously, the quetzal surged up, up, up into the sky!

'*Adios*, Patti!'

For a second he saw her below him waving. Then she was a dot on a field of green. Then the green was a patch in a criss-cross of streets and canals with a white square in the middle. Then the island was a patch in the middle of a lake shaped like a seahorse. Then, as the bird flew higher

142

and higher, faster and faster, the island and then the lake became dots in a skinny bit of land between the bulging shapes of the Americas north and south. But soon he couldn't tell land from sea as outlines faded, and green and blue and white and brown merged and blurred and his head nodded. He was aware only of the bird's wings flapping beside him silently up and down, and the surrounding stars as he moved away from the Earth, through space and time and dimensions he couldn't name.

Then he must have fallen asleep, because when he woke it was light. He felt the sun on his back and Earth was coming towards him. Rapidly. Too rapidly.

'Hold tight, Ka!' They were hurtling towards land, towards a chequerboard of familiar streets, some with huge square buildings getting huger, huger, huger. Some were spiky with TV aerials. One had a spire and a cross on top and he was going to crash into it!

But no, now he could hear the bird's wings.

Whoosh! Whoosh!

The quetzal was pulling back its wings, braking, braking. He felt its taut muscles beneath him as it hovered over something very familiar, a garden and a red brick house. It landed on the ridge of the conservatory beneath his bedroom. In one leap Ka jumped off the bird's back and in through the open window. Topher climbed in after her more carefully – the roof was frosty – then turned to thank the quetzal, but it had gone. He saw it in the sky flying towards a watery sun.

It was morning. His bedroom was cold. The house was quiet. Too quiet. He remembered the night he left. One, two, three, thirty nights ago? It seemed much longer.

'Come with me, Ka.'

She padded after him into Tally's room. Together they stood by the empty cot which still bore the indent of her hot body. He remembered Tenochtitlan, the City of Dreams that became the City of Death. How quickly happiness turned to sorrow. Downstairs the phone rang – and rang. He didn't want to answer it. What if it were bad news?

'Mwow!' Ka nudged his leg. 'Mwow! Mwow!'

'Okay.' He followed her downstairs, and picked up the phone.

It was Ellie. He told her about Tally. She said, 'Remember your name, Topher, HOPE! Doctors can do wonders. We're not living in the Middle Ages.'

Ka rubbed round his legs purring. *She's rrr...ight. She's rrr...ight. Hope, Topher, hope.*

Then the front door opened and his dad walked in looking shattered.

'Dad, is Tally going to be okay?'

He nodded and hugged Topher, and suddenly it was thrilling to be home.

Chapter 25

Tally was fine, well she was by half term when Topher and Ka went to stay with Ellie in London. It was odd being back in Arburton Road with its higgledy-piggledy Victorian roofline and car alarms going off all the time. When he and Ellie walked past Number 35 where he used to live, the dog from Number 58 was peeing against the plane tree, as it always used to do, and it seemed as if time had stood still.

'So Tally really is completely better?' said Ellie.

'Yes.'

'Told you she would be,' said Ellie. 'She's a real little fighter and doctors are getting better all the time. When I got meningitis I went deaf you know, till I had my operation. By the way, did you know that some of the knives brain surgeons use are made of obsidian, just like the knives the Aztecs used for cutting out hearts, etcetera?'

'It's harder than metal so you can get a sharper edge,' said her dad, though Russell, Ellie's brother, was hanging on his arm demanding a swing. 'I hope they have some on show.'

'As long as they're in glass cases,' said her mum. 'I wouldn't like Russell to get hold of one.'

Russell was a bit wild. Mr and Mrs Wentworth both had hold of him now, one hand each, but he was trying to escape. They were all on their way to the Royal Academy to see the new Aztec exhibition. Topher wasn't keen, he'd had enough of the Aztecs, but to his surprise, Ellie was. She seemed to have forgotten her dislike of historical things.

The Northern line was as slow as ever – Topher hated the Tube – but at last they were at the Academy, and Ellie was calling him 'Wimp!' He was hesitating outside the darkened gallery where two huge statues of Aztec gods stood guard. Suddenly he was back on the pyramid steps with statues peering down at him, and though he could hear kids inside the gallery shrieking and laughing, he could smell dried blood.

Ellie tugged at his arm. 'Come *on*! The others have gone in.' She dragged him towards a row of statues. 'That the god of beauty? I don't think so. He looks like a garden gnome! And look at old Goggle Eyes.'

She was laughing at Tlaloc the Rain God, and perhaps he did look funny if you hadn't seen him – or smelled him – caked with blood and swarming with flies. His turquoise face had a big cheesy grin and jug ears, and Tophen felt the goggle eyes following him round the room. As they went round they saw quite a lot of Tlaloc, mostly on drinking or water-carrying vessels. There was tons of stuff – Topher was surprised so much had survived – even feathers hundreds of years old and embroidered clothes and obsidian knives.

'But where's all the gold?' Ellie complained. 'I thought the Aztecs had stacks of it.'

'They did, but the Spanish melted most of it down,

146

and the Aztecs preferred turquoise and jade and feathers and beans, specially cocoa beans . . . '

'I know, Topher. I did the Aztecs too. Come on. Let's look at those masks.'

'But I . . . ' He stopped himself just in time, as Russell appeared saying he'd seen everything and could he go to the shop now.

'I'll take him,' he said quickly as Mrs Wentworth sighed. 'But let's go to the café first, Russell Brussel.'

He'd spotted it on the way in. It was bright and modern and the only sign of the Aztecs was the chocolate at the counter.

He bought them both mugs of hot chocolate and chocolate muffins. Then they went to the shop where Russell bought masks so he could scare his friends, and a rubber ball. Even so it seemed ages before the rest of the family joined them. He took Russell back to the café where he coloured in most of the masks before the Wentworths appeared, having one of their intellectual discussions.

'Brilliant workmanship,' said Mr Wentworth. 'The Aztecs were undoubtedly clever.'

'But so cruel,' said Mrs Wentworth.

'Because of what they believed. They were only doing what their gods wanted.'

'But don't people create gods in their own image?' asked Ellie's mum.

'Then why were Cortes and co. so cruel?' said Ellie. 'I thought Jesus said, "Love your neighbours" and "Do unto others as you would be done by" and "Do not kill". But they were as bad as the Aztecs.'

'Not all of them.' Topher remembered a man with a stillness about him. 'There was one man, a monk called Bartolomé de las Casas, who thought Christianity was all about kindness. If he'd gone to Tenochtitlan with Cortes, things might have been different. Bartolomé had brilliant ideas. He said, "All people are human" whether they're pink, brown or black, which sounds obvious to most people now, but it didn't then. And he was against slavery when it was normal to own people, and work them to death. He was way ahead of his time.'

'So why isn't he famous?' said Ellie. 'I didn't see anything about him in the exhibition.'

'Because good deeds don't make the headlines,' said her dad.

Topher shut up, because Ellie was looking at him as if to say – where did you learn all that? But he wanted to tell her more about Bartolomé, who thought about *people* when everyone else was mad for gold. He'd have liked to tell her about Patti, but wished he knew what had happened to her. He knew that things went from bad to worse after he'd left. He'd read about it. Cortes returned and destroyed Tenochtitlan but returned to Spain and lived to an old age. El Sol didn't. He eventually got his comeuppance, when he fell off his horse in the middle of another battle. Bartolomé wrote a book describing what the Spanish did, in Mexico. It was a famous book for years and years and started to change people's minds, but it wasn't published till twenty years after the fall of Tenochtitlan. The internet was full of info, but didn't say if Patti escaped and got back to her

mum and dad. He wanted to believe that she did, but –
he had to admit – if he had to go back to the time of the
Aztecs to find out, he didn't want to. He'd seen some
amazing things but it was definitely the most horrible
time he'd ever been to.

Ellie broke into his thoughts. 'Cheer up, Topher. You
look as if you're at a funeral.'

When they got back to the Wentworths' house in
Cheverton Road, he went upstairs to check something.
Not Ka, though it was great to see her on his bed with
Duo, her tabby son, washing behind his ears, but a plant
on the windowsill. Ellie found him watering it when she
came in soon afterwards. 'What's this, Topher? Didn't
know you were into gardening.'

'It's an avocado tree.'

'Tree? It's only got two leaves. You didn't bring it
with you?'

'Yup. I grew it myself, from an avocado stone a
Mexican girl gave me, and I thought Molly might forget
to water it.' It seemed very important to keep it alive.

Ellie looked miffed. 'How did you meet this Mexican
girl?'

What could he say? *I helped to rescue her when she
was in danger of being sacrificed? She put the sticky
seed in my hand on the night I left Tenochtitlan?* It
would prove he wasn't a wimp, but somehow he didn't
think she'd believe him. Luckily, Russell the Brussel
came in with a toy mouse on a string, and Ka and Duo
went chasing after it, and Ellie went after them. But Ka
seemed to notice he was feeling a bit low because she

came back a few minutes later. He sat on the bed and she jumped onto his knee.

Don't worry. Don't worry. You'rrre all rrr . . . right.

'And Patti, how's she?'

She's all rrr. . . ight. She's all rrr. . . ight. She's all rrr. . . ight.

'How do you know?'

But if she answered he didn't hear, because Ellie was back, saying there was a good programme on later called 'What Did the Aztecs Do For Us?'

He said, 'I already know what they did for me.' For Ka was looking at him, her eyes full of love, purring like a tractor. He buried his face in her fur. 'They make me ever so glad to be home!'

GLOSSARY & PRONUNCIATION GUIDE

ahuacatl – (a-hoo-a-catl) Avocado, a fruit used by the Aztecs for food and washing

Aztecs – the Indians that lived in central Mexico and ruled over the other tribes

Bartolomé de las Casas – (bar-tol-om-ay day-las-cas-as) a Spanish missionary who tried to protect the Indians

causeway – a strip of dry land built over water

chamberlain – the servant in charge of the keys in noble households

conquistadors – (con-kee-stad-ors) the men who conquered the Aztecs

Cortes – (Cor-tes) Hernan Cortes, the leader of the conquistadors

El Sol – the nickname of Pedro de Alvarado, the conquistador who was Cortes' second in command

De Escalante – the name of the man Cortes left in charge of Veracruz when he went to Tenochtitlan

De Guzman – (day. guth-man) the name of Cortes' chamberlain

Doña Marina – (Donya Mareena) the Spanish name given to the Aztec woman who acted as Cortes' wife in Mexico

Huitzilopochtli – (weets-eel-oh-poach-tlee) the Aztec god of war and sun. He consumed human blood and hearts

jade – a green stone highly valued by the Aztecs

Jeronimo – Cortes' translator, a conquistador who had been a prisoner of the Mayans for two years till rescued by Cortes

Lake Texcoco – (tesh-coco) the lake on which the Aztecs built their island city

major-domo – the servant in charge of the other servants in noble households

Mayan – (my-an) the language of the Mayan tribe of eastern Mexico

Mexico City – the modern capital of Mexico, built on the ruins of Tenochtitlan.

Montezuma – (mo-tek-zoo-ma but commonly called mon-te-zoo-ma) last great ruler of the Aztecs. Reigned 1502–1520

Nahuatl – (na-watl) the language of the Aztecs, still spoken in central Mexico today

Ocelotl – (oc-ee- lotl) jaguar and god of warriors

Otomi – a tribe from central Mexico

obsidian – a shiny volcanic stone like glass used for tools and weapons

patolli – a game played with pebbles and dried beans

quetzal – (ket-sal) a brightly coloured bird

Quetzalcoatl – (ket-sal-ko-atl) the god of knowledge and wind and creation, the most important Aztec god, worshipped by other tribes as well

Tabasco – a tribe in northern Mexico

Tenochtitlan – (tee-noach-teet-lan) capital city of the Aztecs built on island in Lake Texcoco

Teudile – (too-dil-ay) one of Montezuma's chief stewards

Tlaloc – (tla-lok) the god of rain and fertility

tlachtli – (tlach-tlee) a game, played by teams with a rubber ball in a walled court

Tlaxcalans – a tribe of fierce warriors in southern Mexico

Totocalli – treasure house in the middle of the Garden of Birds where Montezuma kept some of his most precious treasures

Totonacs – a tribe in eastern Mexico

Veracruz – (vera-crooth) short for Villa Rica de la Vera Cruz, or Rich Town of the True Cross, a town on the east coast of Mexico

Xocolatl – (shoc-o-latl) food of the gods, chocolate, a frothy drink made by Aztecs from ground-up cocoa beans and boiling water

Xicotencatl – (shee-co-ten-catl) – lord of the Tlaxcalans